SOMMARSTUGA

EMMA WILSON-KANAMORI

AF092766

Phoenix Moirai LLC | Gilbert | Arizona

Phoenix Moirai LLC
1525 S. Higley Rd., Suite 104
Gilbert, AZ 85296
phoenixmoirai.com

Sommarstuga

Copyright © 2025 Emma Wilson-Kanamori

This book is a work of fiction. Any historical events, real names, or real places are used in a fictitious manner. All additional names, locations, or people come from the author's imagination, and any resemblance to actual events, places, or people, living or dead, is entirely coincidental. Trademarks or real company names used have not endorsed this material and no request of such is intended.

First Phoenix Moirai paperback edition February 2026

Original cover art by Bryan Caron
© 2025 by Phoenix Moirai LLC

All Rights Reserved, including the right to reproduce this book or portions thereof in any form for any reason. For information, please inquire to Phoenix Moirai Rights Department, 1525 S. Higley Rd., Suite 104, Gilbert, AZ 85296

ISBN: 979-8-9923079-8-6

Manufactured in the United States of America

To purchase this and other books by Phoenix Moirai LLC, go to https://whimsillusion.com
Whimsillusion logo and design are property of Phoenix Moirai LLC

There are pieces of other, living people's stories that came together and spun this tapestry for me, though I took extreme creative and folkloric liberties. I can safely confirm that staying in a summer cabin in Sweden isn't usually so eventful as this story would imply, but being a young woman in the current state of the world most certainly is.

Thank you, Treacle, for keeping me sane. You came to me with all your fur falling out, and now you're the softest, most loving pillow a girl could ask for, and my incredible soul cat. Thank you also to Clare and Saskia for making me look like a badass in my headshots, and to the team at Whimsillusion and Phoenix Moirai for taking a chance on my freaky little novella.

To the girls who like to eat boys (and other girls).

SOMMARSTUGA

HANA

Hana

My name is Hana. I watched my girlfriend die and come back to life.

Not everyone can say that, right? Trust me, I wish I couldn't either. But on the first night of our summer holiday, I walked in on her sister stabbing her to death. We were in a summer cabin — *Sommarstuga*, the locals called it. A small, idyllic, red-painted thing in the middle of the woody region of Småland. A group of rag-tag college kids on summer break, brought together by the overpowering force that was my girlfriend: Esme Martin. She was still fresh-faced at nineteen years old, with red hair that tumbled in haphazard waves down her shoulders. You could spot her from miles away by the back of her head. We'd only been dating for a couple of months at that point, but it was already difficult to imagine a time and place where Esme Martin *hadn't* been a constant in my life.

And for that one, horrible moment, Esme was gone, and all the ties that bound us to that little cabin flew out the window with her. Until the next, more awful moment arrived.

Esme sat up gasping. I thought her hair had wrapped around her marble-white throat until I realised Alice had sliced it straight across, much like a gratuitous scene out of a horror movie. That would explain how Esme's blood had arced across the otherwise clean, dark countertops. How it had coloured the rustic floorboards, still so fresh that it hadn't melted into suspicious, obscured stains. Of course, it was all across Alice too. Her turtleneck vest, originally a pleasant maroon colour, now had uneven patches of brighter chroma up and down her chest.

"*Fuck!*" Esme shouted, and her hands flew to the severed gash that was her throat. I couldn't really understand how she was speaking, and it took me another moment to fail to understand how she was *alive*. My third instinct, then, was to call the hospital — that vague failsafe in the backgrounds of our lives that was always one phone screen away. Then, with gusto, my fourth instinct arrived to remind me that we had no signal out here. This was a real, back-to-nature getaway — besides which, all of us but one in the group had never set foot in Sweden before in our lives. Alice dropped the knife with a sharp, clean clatter, slicing away any chance of a *fifth* instinct. "You've *got* to be *fucking kidding me*, Alice!"

Alice, bless her heart — or not, as the court of law might judge it — was traumatised from the get-go. Her eyes were the size of commemorative coins, and all the colour had drained out of her face and into the front of her vest. I pushed my feet to move forward, and then forced my knees to drop down beside Esme. I immediately regretted it when I felt her blood squelch up against my kneecaps.

"What happened?" I rasped. Any liquid that had been keeping my throat in working condition had dried up into a pipsqueak of terror. I couldn't look at Esme, so I looked up at Alice. She was a small, slight seventeen-year-old. Not exactly a Ted Bundy, you know? And her eyes were growing larger by the second. "Alice?"

"She fucking *murked* me!" Esme fumed. She looked like a shop mannequin that had been painted a little too realistically. Her skin was too white, at least in comparison to the blood that was soaking her butter-yellow blouse. For some reason, her eyelashes stuck out to me — jet-black spider legs that spread prettily around her blue eyes. The corners of her lips were peeled back, baring ceramic teeth. I suppressed a shudder.

"I'm sorry," Alice said, a little stupidly. She took a step back, then slapped a hand over her mouth. "Oh my god."

I was amazed that the commotion hadn't awoken the rest of our wayward group, but it was a long drive to get here, and a long week in Gothenburg before that. Several of us were falling asleep in the rental car before we were even close to the cabin. To be fair, I'm not sure if more people was what we needed right then. That seems, in hindsight, like it would've just amplified the panic. "Clean her up," I said numbly. Then I reoriented my demand. "Fetch me, like, a wet towel."

Alice numbly obeyed. Now that the expletives had had their hey-day out of Esme's mouth, she seemed suddenly hollow and confused as well. She stared down at the blouse she had been so excited to buy in the city. I felt a hard twinge in my chest.

"She... she tried to —"

"Yeah, I gathered." What else do you say to that? My mind scrambled. Well, there was lots you could say. Lots you could do. I wouldn't have imagined myself being so calm around an attempted murderer. Alice came stumbling back and reaffirmed my lack of fear. Whatever she had done, it had been spur of the moment, and she visibly regretted it. There were obviously going to be far-reaching consequences in the future, but I needed to focus on the present. "Can you — okay, Esme, can you put pressure on the —"

"On my slit throat, Hana?" she drawled with venom. I knew she didn't mean it. She'd never spoken to me that way before. I wish I could say she'd never spoken to *anyone* that way before. "On my — *fuck*. Alice, you tried to kill me."

"I did," Alice said plaintively. There were a few moments of Esme and I wrestling with the already soaked towel before she raised her voice a little more. "I *did* kill you. You didn't have a pulse."

We both paused. On any normal day, that wouldn't have been a good thing to do at such a critical juncture, but this was anything but normal. "What are you on about?" I hissed.

"She was dead. Like, I was about to have a panic attack." Alice may *still* have had a panic attack. She was shaking hard, and I don't think she even realised it. "Does that *surprise* you? She shouldn't be... shouldn't be breathing, let alone *talking*."

Esme looked like she wanted to make another sarcastic retort, but she simply touched her bleeding throat. Her features suddenly smoothed over and she peeled her fingertips away. The blood was congealing, growing cold. In other words, this very obviously fatal wound was no longer actively bleeding.

What. The. *Fuck.*

"Wow," Esme said coolly. "Would you look at that."

I raised my hands in an active attempt to wash them of this fuckery, but then I quickly lowered them again. My heart was beating an entire drum and bass line in my chest. My girlfriend swiped her fingertips irritably on the dish towel, then slowly worked her head from side to side, testing the sinews in her neck. She closed one eye in a sort of *ew* gesture, obviously not liking the feel of the ongoing chasm in her throat. Alice desperately hugged herself, and I could see the goose-prickles lifting up the skin of her arms. "Congrats, Alice. I'm not dead. Somehow."

"That's not normal," I pointed out the obvious. "*None* of this is normal, actually. Alice — what the fuck?"

"I'm surprised you had it in you." Esme was testing the rest of her limbs in haphazard order. She pressed her palms hard against the sticky floorboards, then bent and un-bent her legs. She tried her neck again, and this time her grimace was lessened. My world, meanwhile, was spinning on a tilted axle. I'd never dissociated before, but I was having that out-of-body experience I'd heard so much of. I don't think Alice was doing much better.

"I didn't mean to do that," she said in a wavering voice. "I just wanted you to — stop."

Stop what? I'd obviously walked into something I had no business being in the middle of, but right now, these two needed *something* between them. I looped a commandeering arm around Esme's shoulders, helping her to her feet, which she also gingerly tested. She must have read the confusion on my face because she supplied the context with the same cool, emotionless tone she'd adopted since she'd realised her bleeding had stopped.

"Just a little sibling squabble, Hana. Alice here gets testy when we bring up our home life."

Two spots of bright colour appeared high on Alice's cheeks. She opened and closed her mouth, then rushed to the little kitchen basin to scrub her hands clean of her sister's blood. When she looked down at her turtleneck, her skin blanched again.

"Are you okay?" I asked Esme uselessly. My world was still swimming futilely, and I wasn't wholly convinced that I wasn't dreaming. She pulled a face at the state of her new favourite blouse.

"I'm tired," she said after a moment. "You know, Hana, there wasn't a light at the end of the tunnel. I'm disappointed about that." It took me a second to understand what she meant, and then I didn't know if that was a good thing or a bad thing. I'd never really thought too much about tunnels after death, or what the light at the end might or might not signify. Besides, she clearly wasn't dead. She clearly was fine.

"You're being dramatic," I told her. When I looked closer at her throat, I could see it wasn't at all the gash I'd first imagined it was. It was just a small cut. My mother had, throughout my life, intermittently told me that a lot of the injuries I'd sustained over time looked worse than they actually were. I supposed that this was just another one of those cases. Relief flooded through me, even though I was left uneasy by the whole episode. "You two need some sleep, and — Alice?"

She looked up from the basin. The tap was off, but she was standing there with her fingers dripping the remaining water back into the stainless steel. Maybe Esme's wound looked worse than it actually was, but I think the stricken expression on her sister's face was only a prelude to how awful she truly felt underneath it all. I swallowed back the harsher words that had bubbled to the surface.

"Try not to stab anyone else."

She stared at me like a deer in the headlights. What had even *happened*?

ALICE

alice

My name is Alice. I killed my sister, and she came back to life — just in time for her girlfriend, Hana, to walk into the room and watch me do it.

I stared down at the knife laid over the floorboards. I barely even noticed Hana leading Esme out of the room. I wasn't even really thinking about what would come next. I've heard about all the different ways murderers react after doing the deed, from immediately turning themselves in to keeping the body rotting in the guest room for days. I was an outlier. None of them had to deal with their victim coming back to life. Not that I'd been planning it or anything. I mean, it wasn't, like, premeditated. I used to dream about doing awful things to Uncle Rowan, and yes, Esme was just *the worst*, but they always said your dream self wasn't a reflection of who you really were.

Intrusive thoughts or whatever. You couldn't be held up in a court of law for those.

But I was looking down at the knife. It was long and thin, and the handle was real, polished wood, as rustic as everything else in the cabin. And it was covered in my sister's blood. *I did that.* Nausea welled up from the base of my stomach. Where was the bathroom? I didn't even remember, but I bolted for it anyway. It took an awkward jog into the cramped corridor to see my sister's back receding into the bathroom's tinny white light. Well, I couldn't go in there.

I stumbled back into the corridor, digging my hip into a passing wooden stand with a ceramic vase of fake flowers. At the end of it, I opened a door to a blast of fresh evening air. Finally, I felt almost normal again. The sickness receded in my stomach.

You couldn't fully appreciate the greenness of the place in the evening. The ambient light took the saturation out of it all, leaving it muffled like the velvet at the back of your late mother's jewellery box. I felt the urge to reach out and crush all the blades of grass in my fingers, but I felt like that wasn't something I should be allowed to do. I felt like I should be clapped in irons the moment I stuck my head out of the cabin. I looked down at my knuckles. My stomach flipped again when I saw that a smear of diluted blood was still clinging to the rise and fall of my skin.

I threw up chunks of the miniature cinnamon rolls we'd eaten on the rental down to the woodlands. I tried to be considerate, emptying my stomach behind a spray of tall yellow flowers. What was the point of being considerate, though? I just tried to kill my sister. I just tried to kill Esme.

I just tried to kill Esme.

This didn't feel real.

I tried to think back to the moment I did it. I tried to search for cold calculation or pure accident. Something to exonerate me or sentence me for life. I wanted it all to be crystal clear and logical. I wanted it to be easy. I couldn't pinpoint the *exact* moment, though — it was like someone had drawn gauze over it all; like it was all flushed in scarlet, the same way I flushed her throat. Like someone else had taken my ha—

No, that's a cop-out. It was me. It was me.

Oh, God, it was *me*.

"Alice?"

I spun around in a crouch. I must have looked like a creep. I could only make out her silhouette at first, but I realised it was one of Esme's friends — Elsa Lagerlöf, the Swedish girl; the one who inspired this whole trip or whatever. She was really quiet the whole ride here, but I thought she was pretty. She didn't seem to put any effort into it either. She had a face that I thought the old poets would have loved.

"What is going on?" she asked. She sounded like she had learned her

English accent from the most posh students at college, and also sounded distinctly Swedish. I never had trouble understanding her.

"Nothing. I'm sick. Sorry."

She came closer to me. She'd turned the light in the corridor on and it followed her outside in a drifting yellow haze, spinning highlights into her hair. She half-knelt, surveying my face with her sombre dark eyes.

"You were arguing or something?"

"Yeah, I don't know. Esme was being a cunt."

She didn't flinch at the vulgar language. I was used to throwing it around my friends, but I'd tried to keep my tongue tied around my sister's. "Well... are you okay?" She pulled a knit grey cardigan tighter around herself. It was warm out tonight, but she looked like the sort of person who would always be cold. I tried to smile (it probably came out a grimace) and nodded my head enthusiastically until she got the message. She paused at the door back into the corridor. From the illuminated side of her face, I think she was looking down towards the bathroom. Then, a little hard, she shut the door.

I was completely in the dark. I hugged my knees and tried not to cry. I had no right to cry. I looked at my hands and they didn't feel like mine. I was making excuses in my mind, but I was so sure they weren't.

I went back inside when I thought I heard an animal cry from the trees. It sounded like a dumb, taunting song.

Esmé

My name is Esme. I'm the bitch that got killed. And the worst part is — I'm still me.

I stood under the spray of the too hot shower that was built into the boarded wood wall. It smelled like damp and old rot, distantly, far behind where the eye could see. It was better than smelling my own blood. That had gotten old pretty quick. Hana moved around just out of my periphery, trying to scrub the blood out of my blouse in the sink. It was cute of her, but I knew it was ruined. I stretched my arms out above my head, watching the stream of water course between my fingertips. My skin looked so *smooth* and taut. I'd never noticed how nice it looked before.

Hana was either too shocked to ask what had happened in more detail, or she was avoiding it. I couldn't blame her, either; though, truthfully, I think I reserved the greatest right to be shocked. I hadn't planned to *die*. Why the fuck would I go on holiday to die? I get that some girls are drama queens, but I'm not like that. I wasn't looking to go out in a blaze instead of a whisper, or whatever the saying is. I had too much to live for. Summer, as I had planned it, was going to be a quaint and completely memorable affair. The type of thing you'd read about in cute paperbacks, where the girls in the Regency era used to go down to their old family summer manors. I didn't have one of those, so I bugged Elsa to find us a good summer cabin. Something her friends recommended. It was a *detox*.

Dying is definitely toxic.

"Hana," I snapped. "Put the blouse down. It's not going to magically change colour." She paused, then turned off the tap. With a slow turn about, she leaned her hips against the sink.

Hana was not like anyone I'd ever met. I'd tolerated girlfriends (and boyfriends) before, but she actually was — *genuinely* — someone I cared about. Her mum was Japanese, and I saw Mrs. Baily's resilience reflected in the strong set of Hana's brows and the rich gold of her eyes. She had her black hair held up in a short ponytail, her fringe curling prettily around her temples. I was soft where she was lean. She could run a mile without breaking out of breath, and I was more suited to a palanquin. We complemented each other. She looked at me with open pain and uncertainty, more than I'd ever seen in her. She wasn't particularly open with her feelings. I found that adorable.

"Don't look at me like that," I told her airily. "I'm not dead, am I?"

"It looked like she nearly decapitated you."

I mean, she pretty much had. That was the confusing part.

"Don't be dramatic. It's just a —" I felt my neck for confirmation, but I couldn't clock a thing. I looked down; my naked skin was pink with the stain of blood and the heat of the shower, but otherwise unmarked. Hana noted my confusion and stepped closer.

"What?"

"It must have been a really small cut. Look. It's gone."

I turned to show her, the water running between my breasts, my hair plastered in wet curls down my shoulders. She stared at my neck and her cheeks were a little pink too.

"That's weird. I swear it was properly brutal."

The bathroom door swung open unceremoniously. Joining in the audience for my tits was the girl I was just thinking about. Elsa pursed her lips. "Hi babes," I said. "Mind knocking first?"

"Your sister's outside crying."

"Oh, good. Let it run its course."

Elsa ignored me and looked pointedly toward Hana. "What is going on?"

"They just had a fight," Hana replied tersely, glancing towards me. Her arms crossed defensively over her chest.

"Can you fight quieter?" Elsa stared brazenly at my body. "Is that blood?"

"Shark week."

"Alice had a knife," Hana said flatly.

"You are fucking kidding me." There was no noticeable change in Elsa's tone — but that's Elsa for you. I shrugged and turned back toward the wood boards.

"I was always a heavy bleeder. I hope she satisfied her psycho murderer cravings."

"Esme, your little sister, that you brought along, pulled a *knife* on you." I could feel Elsa glaring daggers into my spine. "Should the rest of us line up too?" I rolled my eyes as I worked the hot water harder over my skin. I didn't exactly want to be blood-coloured for the rest of my life.

"She's a brat. You know I wouldn't have brought her along if *dear papa* hadn't insisted on it."

And insisted on it he had, with his world-wearied look and half his head already in his hands as he asked it. He was a doctor. In our day and age, that was pretty much a mental suicide. Any way he could get his two troublesome daughters off his plate in one fell swoop would briefly alleviate a little of the stress that he was under. I could imagine Alice pulling a knife on me would, frankly, be just another day for him.

"What were you even fighting about?" Elsa asked, her shoulder hitting the doorframe as she slumped with the exhaustion of an interrupted sleep. You know, I wish people would show more concern that, I don't know, I had a *knife* pulled on me. They didn't all have to be like my father.

"Does it matter? Honestly, she's a crazy bitch. Unstable, I think her school counsellor said. She'll probably do weird things like *pick up knives* and *sing lullabies to haunted dolls* —"

"It's not funny, actually."

I glanced over at Hana, waiting for her to back me up. She was staring at her feet, gnawing at her lip. I guess she was processing the trauma of me getting murked in her own special way. I know that she cared, and she was concerned, even if she didn't show it as much on the outside. I turned off the shower and stepped onto one of the towels that she had prepared — some coarse, off-white thing that was probably hand-picked to match the cabin rather than for comfort. I took my time drying down, then wrapped it around myself before turning back to Elsa.

"Relax. She just lost her temper with me. I'm sure she'll think you're too cool and mysterious to pick a fight with."

"Thank you. I feel so much better being stranded alone with an aspiring murderer-to-be now."

I smiled sardonically at her before turning back to Hana. "Thank you for trying to rescue the blouse, babes. That was so cute of you." I made a show of giving her a kiss, hoping that would be enough to disgust Elsa and send her back to bed. I heard a sharp little exhale, then the squeak of her heel turning followed by her soft steps back down the corridor. I giggled against Hana's lips. "God, she's so uptight."

"She has a point, though." Hana's hand came up, cupping my cheek. "It's not actually funny that any of that happened. I think your sister needs some help."

I felt a flash of annoyance and jealousy. Didn't *I* need the help? I was gushing blood just a few minutes ago.

"I told you. She's already got a counsellor. I don't know. I'm not her keeper."

"Right, I get that. But she's still your family, yeah?"

Hana, oh, Hana. I sighed and pulled away.

"I'm going to find my jammies. You'll sleep with me tonight, right?"

"Yeah. 'Course."

That's better. Forget Alice and her issues. Having a knife pulled on me wouldn't seem so bad once I had Hana tucking me in her arms.

Because, luckily, that's all that happened. A knife pulled and nothing more. That's what I was telling myself then.

The cabin had three bedrooms. The one by the bathroom, Elsa shared with Alice. On the opposite end, past the kitchen and the eating area, there were two others side by side. Esme and I had one, and the boys — Cannon, Finn, and Byron — had the next. There'd been a passive aggressive half-squabble about the solitary one by the bathroom. It would be the quietest, most separate, so Esme had assumed that she and I would win it by virtue of being the lovey-dovey couple. Elsa had flatly stated she was not going to sacrifice her sleep to survive the summer next to three rowdy idiots. She was a light sleeper, in case you couldn't tell already.

So, there we were, tiptoeing to our bedroom door so we wouldn't wake the lads. Except they were such heavy sleepers; I could hear Cannon snoring before we'd even cleared the eating room. Esme rolled her eyes expressively in the dark, which my eyes had thankfully adjusted to. There was some unspoken *boys will be boys* affection there, but really, Cannon was her best mate. He could do no wrong by her opinion of him.

Unfortunately for me, I was in no mood for sleeping. Watching your girlfriend get killed will do that to you. And I know I'd seen it, and that I hadn't imagined it. I know my grasp on reality is pretty solid. My mother taught me all she knew in her post-divorce, single mother against the world mentality, and I'd welcomed her bitter grip on life into me with the open and curious heart of a child, which then turned into the no-nonsense soul of a teenage girl who was sometimes the mother instead of the daughter. I admired her, though. She went from surviving a husband who expected her to be submissive and docile on a vague understanding of her culture to a successful businesswoman who was on the board of directors for an established tech conglomerate. She was the closest thing to a role model I had, if an intimidating one to live up to. She never held that over my head, though. Guess that's why I love her.

And I guess that's why Esme and I bonded so well. We met in a particularly rainy spring, frequenting the same second-hand bookstore that was maybe fifteen minutes off-campus, tucked into a bumpy street that most students wouldn't look twice at. I was holding up a copy of Bram Stoker's *Dracula* and she'd swung up to me to say, "Read it — it's funnier than people give it credit for." It had been — and so was she. Funny, vibrant, smart as all hell. She was operating as the eldest daughter of a single-dad family; and with her dad being a doctor, he was as busy and intimidating in her life as my mum. Two eldest daughters bonding from a meet-cute. It was bound to blossom into romance.

So, there I was, in a generous summer cabin in Sweden, after dating this girl for only a couple of months. I grabbed the bull by the horns — would it be the cow by the teats? — and become party to a crime. Not a crime? Esme was alive. We could feasibly say it had never happened. It would be easier. I knew that wasn't how the world worked, though. You couldn't just brush something like that under the carpet. Or under the charming rustic rural floorboards. She fell asleep almost instantly, not caring for her slippery wet hair spread-eagling over her pillow leaving damp streaks whenever she turned her head with a mutter or a sigh. I lay beside her, my eyes refusing to shut, counting each of her now naked, butterfly-soft lashes.

I was glad she wasn't dead.

I turned onto my back, listening to the stillness of the cabin. Really, I was listening to see if Alice had come back inside. I had no heart to go find her and get some long-form confession out of her. Despite everything, I just hoped the kid — I thought of her like that, despite her being only three years younger than me — wouldn't do anything else stupid, like turn the knife on herself. A lot of killers did that, right? Out of guilt, or... wanting to escape ramifications. But also, Esme had said she was 'unstable', which was usually uneducated talk for, *hey, this person I know has pretty serious mental health issues that should've been addressed a long time ago.* That wasn't a far-fetched thought after what I'd seen that night. If she did come back in, though, I didn't hear anything. Which also didn't mean much, since she was on the far side of the cabin with Elsa.

Elsa. I pictured her slumped against the bathroom doorframe. How still her face was when I told her Alice had picked up a knife. Almost like she didn't care, really. I barely knew these people. I barely knew Esme. I'd grabbed the teats and ridden the cow out of infatuation, and what had I landed myself in?

At some point, I closed my eyes. I think I got about three hours of sleep before Cannon Moody's rowdy Texas twang filled the cabin. I hadn't quite figured out yet if he was faking the whole thing. Among a group of Brits, no-one had the know-how to really call him out. It *did* sound exaggerated though.

"Rise and shine, princesses. Breakfast's being served."

He hung in the doorway in an awful white wife-beater, his hair already done ten ways to Sunday with gel. I raised an eyebrow at him until he backed off, then turned to look at Esme. She hadn't woken yet and looked so still, I was afraid, for a moment, that she really *had* died in her sleep; that I'd overlooked her impending demise in my vigil last night. I bent my ear over her mouth, waiting for a gust of warm breath to hit my skin. Nothing came, but I heard an annoyed little grunt.

"That's a weird way to kiss me good morning."

I pulled back, worried. She had opened her eyes, and the drifting morning light made them a lighter blue than they actually were. Without her make-up, she looked strangely small and soft.

"I was just checking you were still alive."

Her forehead wrinkled, though the rest of her stayed still. "Are you still going on about that? Honestly, Hana."

"It's kind of a big deal, Esme."

"Maybe you and Elsa should've gotten a room."

I did often get annoyed at Esme, and this was one of those moments. I never saw it as a deal-breaker that she could be a real bitch sometimes. I kind of admired that in women. Still, it didn't make it any less infuriating when she lived up to that image of her.

"All right, fuck me for caring. I'm going to get breakfast."

"I'll be with you in a minute," she said vaguely. She still hadn't moved. I frowned at her as I stood. I hadn't even bothered to change into my jammies last night since I hadn't been planning to fall asleep.

"You sure you're all right?"

She looked at me openly for a moment, like she was seeing me for the first time. It took me by surprise; lowered my hackles. The corner of her mouth curled up.

"You're a worry-wart, babes. Just go and get some breakfast. I'll catch up."

I didn't really want to. I wasn't hungry, picturing her blood spattering the kitchen last night. Wait — her blood in the kitchen. Nobody had bothered to clean that up, had they? I felt the room spin a bit from my dual anxiety.

"All right," I said, distracted. "Don't be long."

We probably didn't deserve Finn Armstrong. Probably because I didn't know him as well as the others. We'd agreed to take turns making the meals of the day and it looked like he'd volunteered for first up, first served. The aromas of an English breakfast powered through the dining area, which was now lit up with the brilliant, green-hued morning light of rural harmony. On any other morning, I'd have inhaled those scents and fallen in love with whomever had produced them. That day, I marched straight past the half-full table and into the kitchen.

Finn looked taller than anyone had the right to be. Though he was an even height with Cannon, he seemed longer, somehow. I think it was the length of his neck. A tight cluster of dark 4C hair was cropped near to an open and smiling face. He'd found an apron somewhere, off-white like the bathroom towels. I tried to reconcile the sight of him there — looking like a cottage-core husband — with the fact that there were obvious dried blood spatters on the wooden counters he was using. The rest of our group hovered in and around, helping out sometimes, broken off and chatting at other times. I couldn't see Elsa or Alice, but Cannon was leaning against one of the counters, chatting up Kaida Gotou — Japanese like me, a little less diasporic. She was always bubbling with a genuine, excited energy. Her hair was sleek and unruffled like black silk in the burgeoning daylight.

"Hana!" she cried out. "Good morning! Did you sleep okay?" I eyed her — and Cannon too — like an injured bird who'd just bumped into two smug cats. I turned my round-eyed gaze to Finn.

"Yeah," he said, shovelling stick-straight sausages onto an inoffensive plate. "We was gonna ask you what happened."

"Who cut themselves with the knife?" Cannon drawled, gesturing like it was the dumbest mistake anyone could make. My shoulders relaxed slightly. They just thought it was a stupid little accident. Maybe it was easier for them to handle in the morning like that.

"Um. Esme and Alice —"

"*Course* it was Esme." Cannon cut me off like he'd known the truth the whole time. Why ask then, dude? "She all right?"

"Yeah, she'll be along." I was distracted because I'd just collided with someone. It was Byron, shorter than me by, like, a few inches with the face of someone who had never quite hit puberty. He blinked up at me. There was a stagnant boyishness in the rosy hues of his cheeks and the uncertain squirming of his mouth. He mumbled an apology. I blinked back to the others. "Where's Alice?"

Cannon was blanking. Finn piped up. "I don't think she's up yet. How many sausages d'you want?"

"Uh. Two. What about Elsa?" There was no way she wasn't awake with all this commotion. Finn levelled his deep brown gaze at me, sensing that something was amiss, but also sensing that I didn't want a huge scene. See? We don't deserve Finn Armstrong.

"Think she was outside smoking a cigarette." It didn't look like he knew that for sure, but it looked like he was giving me an out. I flashed him a quick, thankful smile, bumped into Byron again, and wound my way back to the dining area. I glanced into our bedroom as I retraced my steps, but Esme had closed the door once I'd left. I tried not to be overbearing and moved onwards.

Elsa *was* outside smoking a cigarette. Lucky guess. She looked up tiredly when I came out of the door, seeming unsurprised by my presence.

"So," I began, and her slender brows inched up.

"Yeah. They think it was an accident."

"I guess it kind of was?"

Elsa sucked hard on the cigarette, then took her time blowing out a bride's veil of smoke. "Do you ever get so angry you *accidentally* try to murder someone?"

I got irrationally annoyed at her. *She* hadn't been there when it happened. I'd've gladly traded places with her if she wanted to know it all.

"Listen. Alice barely touched her. It might be best just to let them think that."

"Okay." She didn't put up a fight. She really didn't care. I squinted at her, trying to make sense of this... inertia of hers. It was like someone had her at gunpoint to be there on summer vacation. Woe is her.

"Esme is okay, by the way."

"Great."

"What's with the attitude, exactly?"

Finally, a stirring of life. She looked at me with her big round eyes, the shadow of a sleepless night beneath them, and sucked in her cheeks with thought. She then huffed, sort of bemused.

"I am not a people person, Hana. That's why I'm smoking outside. Alone."

Why were she and Esme even friends? They were so... different. I shrugged, feeling like an idiot, but knowing that I wasn't.

"So — we're cool?"

"On not telling them what happened? Sure."

I didn't like how she put it, but I didn't exactly want to cultivate further conversation with her. I started to turn back, then stopped.

"Hey, where's Alice?"

Elsa had looked away, scanning the distant trees that marked the beginning of the nearby woods. "She doesn't want to get out of bed."

Esme

When we were younger, Alice asked me once if I ever had trouble remembering to breathe. I guess someone had planted it in her head, all crinkled with worry, so she planted it into mine in turn. It was all a huge con, because making you think about it made it harder to breathe, which deepened the worry that maybe, just maybe, you might *really* forget.

I lay in the four-poster feeling sorry for myself because it felt like I had to remember to breathe. It felt like I hadn't slept; all I remembered were the murky shapes of nightmares. I was on a walk through the woods and this girl kept walking behind me, but she would stop when I stopped, and she would run when I ran — how fucked is that? And when I opened my eyes, I expected it to still be in the wee hours of the morning, but instead, everyone was up, and Hana was listening to see if I was still breathing.

Do you ever have trouble remembering to breathe?

I didn't feel ill, exactly. I didn't even feel physically exhausted, per se. It was like a great mental depression, where it took a lot of effort to direct all my different limbs to move in different directions. My eyes were dry and scratchy and didn't want to close up again. I was unsettled and at peace at the same time. Once, when I lifted my arm to the morning light, I admired the perfection of my skin again. I swore I used to have more freckles or something. Curse of the redhead, right?

Purposeful footsteps glided past the closed door. I inhaled sharply and then finally sat up. I *wasn't* going to spend my summer holiday feeling like a piteous damsel. A wafting scent of cooked sausage meat billowed through the little gap under the door and my stomach turned with a heady hunger I hadn't experienced since childhood. "All right, you cunt," I said to myself. I had satisfaction in denigrating my prone, sulking form. "Rise and shine."

You remember how I said the worst part of it all was that I'm still me? I felt that empty dissatisfaction as I stood up, too. Like, somehow, I wanted to have undergone a great and fulfilling change as a result of the quarrel last night. I wanted something to show for it all, like an ugly scar or a new stretch of skin altogether. Looking down at my hands, I imagined myself looking into a mirror and pulled a face. I would need to fix myself up before I showed myself in front of the others. It was all about setting the tone for the whole week. I felt as though if I went down there with a naked face, they'd all make me a target. They'd whisper behind my back and have great satisfaction doing so.

I opened the door slowly, looked up and down the little corridor that led out of the dining area and paved the way to the two bedrooms. The bathroom was all the way past the breakfast rabble. I rolled my eyes and shut the door again. After digging in my travel bag, I unearthed one of those vintage compact mirrors sculpted to look like a seashell. It was a gift from my dad for my fifteenth. The card had said, *Happy birthday to my little Ariel, xx.* I opened it up and eyed myself critically in the small circular dome. I was one of the girls who looked 'mature' for nineteen. Older guys as young as sixteen would hit on me and claim they had no idea I wasn't thirty. Rude, and honestly unbelievable. I prodded at my pale cheeks and the discoloured area under my eyes that said I hadn't slept well. All right then. It was time to do the grisly work.

I had just finished swiping concealer under my waterline when I heard a tentative knock at the door. It wouldn't surprise me in the least if it was Hana coming to make sure I lived up to my promise. Worry-wart.

"Come in," I called out in drawling sing-song, squeezing a little bit of rosebud pink blush onto the tip of my pinky finger. The door swung inward and haggard little Alice stood in its empty frame, wavering on her feet.

"Hi," she said. She looked in fixed fascination at the small seashell compact, then at my reflection inside it. I watched her through it likewise, pursing my lips.

"Haven't come to finish the job, have you?"

"Please don't joke about that. I'm really sorry."

I lifted my eyebrows and continued patting the blush onto the highs of my cheekbones. Every so often, I would irritably swipe a dangling ginger curl off of my face. "I don't want to keep talking about it. You just had a little coo-coo episode, like you always do —"

Alice bristled. "Please stop calling me crazy."

"You aren't doing yourself any favours, you know."

Alice gnawed on her lip. She let her hand drop from bracing itself on the doorjamb, then carefully stepped inside of the room. What was she? Afraid I'd stab her back? *Honestly.*

"I don't know what came over me. You just — *really* pissed me off. And I thought you'd understand about Uncle Rowan —"

"I don't want to talk about him, either."

"So, we're just not going to talk?" Her eyes were round and desperate. Where I'd inherited our mother's softness, she was all sharp angles like our father. Eyes too large for her small, pointy face. A cute little perky nose. I wonder if Uncle Rowan looked down at her at night and saw his own brother. No. I don't want to think about that either. I snapped the compact shut and turned to look at her with a flare about my nostrils.

"I'm sorry, okay? I'm sorry for being a stuck-up bitch. There. Are you happy now?"

"No, I — *I'm* the one who picked up a knife. I tried to... to *hurt* you..." Alice faltered. She was staring at my neck, more openly now than when she was studying me through the seashell mirror. "Where... wait, where'd the cut go?"

"What cut?" I sniped flippantly. I liked watching her squirm. I deserved a little fun after being not-killed, you know.

"*Esme.* I sliced your throat! I don't even know how you're not bedridden. Can I...?"

I cringed and recoiled when she tried to get closer, like I was a live specimen in one of her bio studies. She froze in place, the colour leeching from her complexion once more.

"It was a little cut, and it looked worse than it was. *God*, don't be such a drama queen, Alice."

"What?" Her voice was tiny and confused. I felt an irrational surge of anger.

"Politely, could you fuck off and feel sorry for yourself with someone else? I'm starved." Never mind that I was the one who'd been feeling sorry for myself just minutes before. Never mind that I could have just gone straight into the kitchen, but I was trying to fix my face like that would fix the hollowness that had formed inside of me since last night. I was just lashing out and taking it out on Alice, like I always did.

I always did that, huh?

Alice's bottom lip scrunched inwards, then she turned away. She made sure to slam the door before she left. I remember I loved doing that when I was seventeen, too, just to make sure my dad felt worse than he already did when he came home from his shifts.

I think I always ended up hurting myself more.

ALICE

Alice

The main attraction of a summer cabin, it turns out, is its complete disconnect from the rest of society. If you went far enough under the trees, you could squint out across an adjacent meadow and see other red-planked huts spattering the distant horizon. You *knew* people were there, but you didn't have to see them every day. You got the tranquil solitude of nature without the terrifying anxiety that you were the only person who existed. I think I might have enjoyed it, at least for the first few days, but all I could think about was what I had done. It went beyond Esme making fun of me for being some self-flagellant martyr. I had never pictured myself capable of ever hurting anyone the way I had been hurt. The way Esme hurt other people. I watched her friends orbit around each other with tinny laughter and superficial jokes, and I felt like the worst of the whole lot of them.

Esme was not a good person. She used to boast to me, in private, how much dirt she had on every one of her friends. Didn't even have to be just friends. I know for a fact that she started off as Cannon's plug, though I've no idea who else she got the drugs from. When he became reliant on her for it, she was delighted. I think she confused him being hooked on pills with him being hooked on her. I guess it enhanced her self-worth. You wouldn't be able to tell it from them on the surface because Cannon was high-functioning — and when he *didn't* function, everyone just thought he was being the weird American.

So, it took exactly one day for him to produce a bag of weed. He brought it out on the first night and announced it was for *true detoxification*, whatever that meant. If it was what I made it out to be, I guess he was detoxing every week. Regardless, it made him seem fun and cool. I know Finn was into it, and Kaida thought it was cute and scandalous. Esme smirked in a corner and smoked along with them like she was an expert. No one asked if I wanted a joint because I was the baby of the group. I didn't want one anyway. All I could think of was how fucked in the head Cannon Moody must be from all the drugs.

When the nightmares started, at least, there was a scapegoat.

"Man, I had the worst trip," Finn was saying at breakfast. This morning, Cannon had stepped up to the challenge. He thought grilling burgers was a great way to start off the day, so no one was really looking forward to it. "Just absolute nightmares all night. Anyone else?"

"Must have been a crap bag of weed," Cannon drawled. He hadn't had the energy this morning to haphazardly style his hair, so it stuck up at odd, fluffy points, the colour of corn flour. Esme hadn't come out of the bedroom yet. She was always a morning person, so it was odd that she was struggling to get up two days in a row. Not odd to me, I guess, knowing what had happened. I sat quietly on a chair drawn up to the kitchen island, picking at the dried blood that someone had missed with the growing edge of one fingernail. "I swear I heard an animal out there in the woods. Do you get coyotes in Sweden?"

"Nah," Finn said automatically. A beat later, he suggested, "You could ask Elsa?"

Elsa had been tossing and turning all night in our shared bedroom. She slept on the floor while I had the all too spacious double bed. I think she went out to smoke at least three times, and she came back shivering like she'd seen a ghost on the third. Maybe she heard the not-coyotes too.

"Where is she, anyway?"

"Outside smoking, probably."

The blood was coming off in flakes like dry skin. I was desperate to be completely rid of it. I convinced myself I was thinking of the person who owned the cabin. They'd be cringing already renting it out to a group of college kids. No need to add blood splatters on top of it.

"Alice?"

I looked up. Finn was looking at me with kind concern, his head tilted in a way that reminded me of a particularly neighbourly magpie. My cheeks coloured and I dropped my hand.

"Sorry, what?"

"I was just wondering if you had any nightmares as well?"

He was asking just to include me. He knew I hadn't shared any of the joints. I hesitated.

"Yeah."

His eyebrows lifted. I think he had more hair in them than Cannon had in all his attempt at growing stubble. "Maybe it's the ghosts of the Swedish woods." He did a ghostly *oo-ooh* hand gesture, and I smiled despite myself. While Cannon struggled with the grease off his frozen burgers, Finn scooched his chair closer to me. "What'd you dream about? I saw this girl in the woods. Proper *Ring* style, if you know what I mean."

I did, yeah. I glanced critically down at the dried blood embedded under my fingernail. "A snake?" I posited, then realised there was no way he could answer me. It was *my* nightmare. "Like there was this giant snake watching me sleep. It wrapped around the posters of the bed and everything." I paused. "Do you get *snakes* in Sweden?"

"Christ, I hope not." Finn leaned his chin into his hand, squinting at the opposite wall. "I guess it's a bit ominous, staying in a cabin in the middle of nowhere. We've probably just got the jitters."

"Yeah."

"You're starting college soon, right?"

"Yeah, hopefully."

He gave me a disarming grin. "Just between you and me, you'll have better outings in the years to come. I'm more for having a pint somewhere and just a simple takeaway, you know what I mean? Goes easier on the wallet."

"And where's the fun in all that?" Cannon drawled. He'd finally managed to scrape one of the burgers free of the bottom of the pan. There was an unappetising, rust-coloured crust atop it. Esme had dirt on Finn, too, though I didn't really think it was *dirty*. She'd dropped enough hints to me that Finn had a thing for Cannon. Finn had feelings for Cannon, Cannon had feelings for Esme, Esme had moved on — it was a long string like fairy lights, but all freshly tangled from coming out of the box. I felt guilty for thinking about it when Finn was being so kind to me.

"It's less about the fun and more about the —" Finn never got to finish that sentence. There was a building drumbeat of heavy footfalls, and we all paused to look at each other as though we'd let in a rhinoceros. There was a blur of wavy red hair and Esme suddenly snatched the greasy pan from Cannon's hands. She crouched over it on the floorboards, shovelling scalding burgers into her mouth, spilling crumbs upon the already stained wood. Cannon leapt back, clutching his chest like he'd had a heart attack. Several of the other prepared plates went crashing to join Esme on the floor.

"What the *hell*?" he demanded, but my sister wasn't paying him any mind. I saw the glitter of her dark blue eyes, staring vacantly ahead as she shovelled as much meat as she could chew between her teeth. She hadn't bothered to make herself up today; she had the pallor of our mother at her open coffin. Hana came careening in after her girlfriend, drawing up short when she saw her bunched up over herself on the floor. There was a mixture of disgust and awe on her features.

"Esme?" she prompted, but Esme wasn't letting anything distract her from the meal at hand. Only once there were crumbs of meat left, shining grease stains ribboning across the floorboards, did she lift her head and stare at us in incomprehension. Her forehead furrowed in annoyance, like we'd placed her in a zoo. "*Esme*," Hana tried again, and my sister's head jerked to one side.

"Oh... what?"

We all held our breaths, waiting for her to come to a conclusion herself. She looked down at her knees squished to her chest and frowned at her filmy fingers. Then, she gagged.

"*Eugh*! Cannon, those burgers taste like charcoal."

Cannon ruffled his hair in reassurance, but looked on the edge of pulling it out, too. "Wow. Really?"

"God. How many did I eat?"

"Um. A handful," Finn provided. He hadn't quite torn his eyes away from the grease streaks. Hana hovered at the edge of the room like she didn't want to step in anything squelchy. I slowly slid my naked feet down onto the wood.

"Are you... okay?" I asked. Her eyes snapped to me, bright and empty. I'd never seen her like this before. Not even on her worst periods. I think she was starting to understand what she'd done, and I know that she hated people ogling her like she was some kind of freak. She pursed her lips hard, then glared around at all of us like we'd caught her naked.

"*Wow*," she snapped. "Can't a girl just be hungry?"

Esme

It wasn't like any hunger I'd ever felt. I *needed* to fill my stomach, and it could have been anything. Anyone. I felt the saliva bursting through my lips from the moment I woke up and Hana was lying next to me. I paid attention to all the spots where I knew blood pooled in a human body. Even as I was eating the charred burger meat, all I could think of were the rosy parts of her skin and how the texture of it would feel against my tongue. I felt my abdomen clench around its new additions, and *God*, it wasn't satisfied. Just a few measly burgers? I wanted to run out into the woods and bury my teeth into something with a thumping heart.

I didn't even *need* to run out into the woods.

I wiped and wiped at my mouth with the backs of my hands, feeling repulsed by the stringy meat stuck between my teeth. There I was in my little heart print jammies, half my hair in my mouth alongside the burger meat, making a proper mess of myself and everything around me in front of everyone around me. I could barely look at the boys and couldn't look Hana in the eye. I glared at Alice, but she was no help. I didn't want to be around them, I decided. And it was probably for the best if I wasn't.

"Now where are you going?" Cannon called after me in exasperation, but I ignored him. I marched through the dining area and found sanctuary in the bathroom. This time, I locked the door. I swiped strands of hair out of my mouth and then, by impulse, I bit into my finger. I didn't even cry out.

I let my teeth sink into the measly flesh there; felt the blood bubble round my gums. I heard a long time ago that if your body doesn't get the nutrients it needs, it cannibalises itself. Once the fat is gone, it starts on the muscles. Keeps going until you're a husk. It's delaying the inevitable, of course, that you're going to die.

Was I dying?

I wrenched my teeth out of my finger and, of course, that's when the pain hit me. I moaned and slid down the door, cradling my hand and rocking back and forth, cursing and hating myself. Why *me*? Why on summer holiday? Why the fuck did Alice *stab* me? It was all interconnected, right, somehow? Because nothing had been the same since I'd sat back up in a fountain of my own spewing blood. Because I felt cold to the marrow, and it felt like my joints had turned to rusted steel. Now my stomach didn't know how to digest what I'd just eaten, and I could feel the over-cooked meat wrenching itself back up through my oesophagus —

I reached the toilet bowl just in time. Absolutely fucking smashing.

It was like I was emptying the last vestiges of my life into that ceramic hell-scape. Purging my body for its new beginnings. The water became dark and murky with burger meat and meals from the day before. I slid back once I was gasping up air. It now felt like all my limbs had turned to stone. I felt completely like a husk — like someone could flatten me with a fly swatter. Maybe it was just a summer flu. Maybe *I* was overreacting now, too.

I wanted to eat them. All my friends, standing around gawking at me in the kitchen. My sister. My girlfriend. I wanted to taste their blood. The very thought of it made the saliva thicken again in my mouth.

What the fuck was wrong with me?

Hana

The funny thing about a friend group that revolves around one person: once that one person starts acting weird, we're suddenly like a group of preschoolers left to our own devices in the middle of a highway. Breakfast had gone completely tits up, so both Kaida and Finn tried to compensate by making two separate versions of it that only they ended up eating. Byron made numerous movie references that nobody listened to, because nobody had seen the movies he was referencing. Elsa became the greatest chain-smoker that I, personally, had ever witnessed. You could tell exactly where the perfect vantage point of the woods was, because it was marked by a growing fairy circle of discarded nicotine butts. The problem was, whenever you went out to said vantage point, you realised what an awful idea this whole 'summer getaway in a rural cabin' thing had been from the start.

Sure, I was pretty new to this particular social circle, but I could already see that half of them had nothing in common with the other half. Elsa probably hated everyone's guts, and nobody knew what to do with Alice. Finn and Cannon were great buds, sure, but Kaida followed them around like a lost puppy because she couldn't hold up a consistent conversation with anyone else. Byron just looked like he was in constant torture. He suggested board games at least five times before anyone took him up on it. By that point, we were all anxious and bored out of our minds.

And where was Esme during this whole debacle? After shutting herself away in the bathroom, she hid away in the bedroom. She didn't answer anyone who knocked, and when I tried the door handle, it was stuck, like she'd propped something up against it from the other side. That was pretty worrying on its own, but I'm ashamed to admit it came pretty low priority after several other things that had happened — like me witnessing a crime, and then her turning into the world's most inelegant carnivore, in that order. So, I walked with low morale back into the dining area, which had been cleared away to become, well, the board game area.

I'd barely shared two words with Byron since I'd been introduced to him months ago. Aside from looking a gangly fifteen, he had the palest eyes I'd ever seen in a person. Your attention span would slowly spread out from there, taking note of the cherub-y white cheeks that seemed to have a consistent case of rosacea, a general harmless, downward slope of the brow area, and a thin-lipped mouth perpetually set in a half-grimace that you could *almost* hear say, "Well, here we are then." That turned out to be his reception towards our situation — *Well, here we are, so let's make the most of it.* And that, in turn, began to endear him to me.

He roped us in with Trivial Pursuit, which I think he didn't particularly care for, but he was trying to appeal to a wider audience. The group of us sat glum and wary of one another in a haphazard circle and, to his credit, became more and more lost in the game, which meant that we were contentedly distracted from our woes at hand. Did we even, God forbid, share a few jokes among one another? Kaida's overexcitement was actually infectious, and I found her squeaks of *ah!*'s and *oh!*'s whenever she got an answer right rather endearing. And I couldn't believe my eyes when Elsa Lagerlöf *laughed*. It was Cannon who made her do it, with his stupid exaggerated drawl that, for once, turned self-deprecating. It didn't take him long to break out the alcohol, either. The bottle rather patriotically stated that it was *Swedish vodka*, which I had no idea how to authenticate, so we took it at its word. He made us up a cocktail that he called *Peach on the Beach* (again, no idea if he came up with that himself or what), and it was after a glass of that that we got really, *really* loud.

We were on a game of Taco Goat Cheese Pizza when Esme finally came out of her room. She hadn't changed out of her jammies, which were speckled with coquettish dark hearts. She stood in the doorway without us noticing her for roughly a minute or two because we were all haphazardly slapping at cards in a way I don't think fell within the rules of the game. My breath was fizzing with peach, peach, peach, and I was just starting to think this whole summer cabin thing was maybe — just maybe — going to work out.

"Careful you don't get too drunk," Esme said. She never raised her voice, but God, it carried through the room like a knife. "Don't want Cannon to have to go back to rehab."

It was a record scratch. The air was completely vacuumed out of the room. Cannon, who had been grinning broadly, his blonde hair flopping over one brow like a golden retriever, saluting us all with a sloshing glass of what looked like melted orange sherbet, seemed to lose control of all of his fingers. The drink careened straight down into the pile of cards, leaving them not only soggy, but decorated with diamond-shaped shards of glass. None of the rest of us knew what to say. Kaida failed to subdue a hiccup.

"Rehab?" Finn said finally, his eyes wide and lost. Only five minutes ago, he'd been egging Cannon to down his drink all in one go. Elsa was quietly cradling the entire vodka bottle all to herself. She pushed it away from her and it slid loudly across the floor like an unleashed marble. Cannon hadn't taken his eyes off of Esme.

"Yeah," he said finally. "I mean. It wasn't much of anything."

"Thirty-day stay," Esme chimed in evenly. "You dressed up as Lindsay Lohan for Halloween that year."

Cannon swallowed and, finally, lowered his hand. Elsa looked between him and my girlfriend in a vague stupor. "What the fuck?" she slurred. "You didn't mention this."

"I just thought it was my own business." The Texas drawl faltered, but not out of anger. I hadn't seen him that deflated in our entire acquaintance-ship. I had mixed feelings myself under the gauze of intoxication. Like, what the fuck? He shouldn't be drinking if he had to go to rehab. And my girlfriend shouldn't have announced that like she was announcing the next bus stop on the ride. She stood still in the doorway, her arms hanging down her sides like heavy pendulums. Byron was quietly scooping the glass off the soaked cards.

"It kind of is," I said finally. "Esme, where've you been?" When her eyes landed on me, I saw her mouth twist with contempt.

"Where've *I* been? Where you *left me*, Hana. I guess no one thought *I* wanted a drink?"

"We thought you were sick," Kaida said hesitantly. She had one hand over her mouth, as though that might subdue any other hiccup that would rise to the occasion. Her dark eyes peered sheepishly over the top.

"I can see how worried you all were," Esme snipped. "Can you at least keep it down so I can sleep?" It seemed redundant to ask, since all our festivities had already come to a screeching halt. The only consistent sound was the clinking of glass in Byron's palm. I felt myself grow annoyed with her. I'd've checked on her if I could — if she hadn't boarded up the bedroom door, or *whatever* she'd done. That, and I couldn't get her *contempt* out of my head. Maybe I'd imagined it. I *was* drinking, after all.

I guess that was a bit selfish, wasn't it? Drinking while she was sick.

"We'll keep it down, Esme," Finn said as warmly as he could given the awkward circumstance. He flashed her a smile that went unreturned. "We can always do this again too, aye? When you're feeling better? Was probably just bad weed."

The consolations came in on cue. Kaida was already on her feet, fussing over Esme. Byron was mumbling apologies as he shuffled the handful of broken glass into the nearest trash bin. Alice remained with her eyes sealed on the wet spot on the floor where Cannon's cocktail had landed. I could imagine she was remembering something else.

It was impressive, really, how quickly Esme instilled shame in all of us. And she didn't even have to change out of her pyjamas.

There was no noise to keep down for the rest of the night. We all drifted apart again, un-tethered by Esme's interruption just as easily as we'd been tethered by the board games scattered about the cabin. I wondered if this was why none of them seemed to get along. It appeared a normal thing for them to have to tiptoe around my girlfriend's sensitivities. I, for one, had never seen that side of her before. But then again, I'd never really seen her around other people for an extended period of time. I kept thinking about her contemptuous look. It was so jarring. She'd never looked at me in that way before, either. If she had, I don't think I would have ever come along on this cursed summer trip.

"It's not you," Alice said hesitantly. I had zoned out, I guess, by the kitchen island. I was drinking water before I went to bed. I think I was stalling, seeing as I shared it with the party pooper of the night. I blinked in confusion at the slight girl only a couple years my junior. She was hovering in the doorway, looking like she regretted speaking up. "She's good at making you think you've done something wrong. You didn't, though. You were just having fun."

Alice had been avoiding being alone with me, I think. I don't think there's a lot two people can say to one another after witnessing one person trying to kill someone else. I still didn't quite know what to say. Her hand dropped from the doorjamb, and she looked set to scurry back into her little mouse hole. I put down my water.

"Is she like that often?" I asked. "Not sick, I mean, but —"

"Awful?" Alice supplied. "Demeaning?"

"That's a bit strong."

"I think she's sweet to you, if that's what you're asking. Honestly, I think she was jealous that you were with us and not with her."

"She barred the door so I couldn't get in. Otherwise..."

"Did she?" Alice's pale brow furrowed. "Well, that's new."

"I guess she must really not be feeling well." I felt self-conscious saying that, after I realised who I was talking to. Then again, I was right to shame her for pulling a knife on someone. That's not exactly a habit you want to condone. Alice hesitated, then her fingers gripped the doorjamb again with renewed intensity. Her eyes bored into me.

"I left — I mean, I really cut into her, didn't I? I didn't make that up, right?"

That's a question that wouldn't have been on my bingo card for the summer. I inhaled slowly. She was a lot thinner than Esme; maybe a little unhealthily so. It was a wonder she could do so much damage with such a small knife. "I thought you did, yeah." Clearly she hadn't actually, because there wasn't a mark left on Esme's neck. Not even a tiny scratch to explain all the bleeding.

Alice's jaw set. I could almost hear her teeth grind. "You *thought* I did, or you *saw* me do it?"

"I mean, she's clearly fine. Whatever it was…"

"What?" she challenged, in that petulant way everyone younger than me seems to do nowadays. I inhaled again, deeper this time.

"I don't know, Alice. Just a fluke. She said she's a heavy bleeder, right? Looks worse than it is and all that."

"*Looks worse than it is* is when you scrape the skin off your knee where it looks like someone took a grater to your kneecap. Or when a papercut bleeds down to your knuckle. When have you seen a papercut splatter blood all over the kitchen?"

I didn't like what she was getting at. In my defence, I don't think anyone would take too kindly to having the very fabric of reality questioned. Because what was the alternative? That it had been *more* than just a tiny scratch, and Esme had healed up in about ten minutes? That's practically fictional. "Clearly I saw it happen here," I said, gesturing vaguely about the kitchen in question. "Clearly you did, too. You should be glad that was all it was, Alice. God, what if you'd *actually* killed her?"

And there it was, the very heart of our crisis. For a moment in time, the both of us *had* thought Alice had killed her. I think the ugliest part of it all was that, in that timeline, things would have been simpler — even *easier*. Alice Martin slit her sister's throat. I watched Esme die in the kitchen and neither of us stood there questioning our reality. We'd call it quits from the summer cabin early, go home, and I'd probably never hear from any of them again. We'd be free of this tense, limbo-esque, so-called holiday where we couldn't even play board games and get a little drunk without feeling like, somehow, we'd twisted the very same knife back into my girlfriend's neck.

Alice huffed through her slender nose. She didn't buy my conviction that everything was fine — just fine. Well, screw that. The alternative was thinking my girlfriend was a zombie. Couldn't she see how selfish that was? How royally fucked up?

"I already feel like I did," Alice said. "I'd rather —"

"Don't say it."

Her eyes flashed, like I was being selfish too. "*Fine*. Good night, Hana."

I didn't answer her back. What a fucked-up summer this had become. I felt exhaustion flood through me and, suddenly, facing a shared bed with a resentful partner didn't seem so bothersome anymore.

Mental exhaustion and the alcoholic peach fizz sent me careening into a heavy sleep. Thankfully, the bedroom door was no longer barred. Esme had her back turned to me in what looked like a deep slumber of her own when I snuck in. I did feel guilty as I slid under the covers, like I was the wayward husband who'd kept his wife waiting up until after two in the morning because I couldn't say no to one more drink with a work colleague. Once my head hit the cool linen pillow, though, that shame she had been so good at instilling evaporated into the marshmallow fuzziness of vague, half-remembered dreams. In them, I smelt the damp forest floor of Småland and I felt the sharp grass of the meadows pierce between my toes. There was a girl crying, or was it a baby, or was it the keening of something more animal? I ran and I ran and I knew I had to make it to the other end of the meadow, far away from the woods. When I looked back, Esme was watching me from between the trees, screaming and screaming and screaming. The air was heavy in my chest, like my ribcage was being crushed from the pressure of pumping my legs on and on. The pain only ballooned as the substance of the dream started to fade and dissipate at its edges. I could smell the damp in the wood walls instead. I could hear the rustling of wind outside the cabin. My arms lifted as though to physically push the weight of exertion off my lungs and then made contact with soft skin and bony knees.

I opened my eyes. Esme was crouched atop of me, baring her teeth in a wide-eyed grin.

I'd like to think I'm not a violent person, and I'd also like to think I was generous in trying to shove her off rather than start kicking and screaming. You never realise the weight of another person until they're crushing you like that — even lifting them up high seems different, somehow. I did start hollering for her to *get off, get off, get off*, and somewhere in the midst of that, she jumped backwards like one of those tiny spiders that people keep as pets. It was so distinctly inhuman that I remembered, in passing, that I had dreamt of an animal crying in the woods.

"*Fu*-cking *hell*," I said, up and down along with the incredibly aggressive beat of my heart. I had rolled off the side of the bed and grasped for the light switch. Esme remained crouched at the end of the bed like a vaguely bemused frog. When the light flicked on, straight into her staring eyes, she flinched and lifted a hand like I'd struck her. "What are you doing? What was that?" I clutched my sternum, which felt bruised and sore, and she peered at me between the slats of her fingers.

"What?"

"What do you mean '*what*'? Don't do that. Don't ever do that."

We stared at one another, and I couldn't help but wonder after the earlier altercation just how many times one of her friends had simply told Esme, *no, don't*. Rather than be affronted, she looked mousily confused. As she grew in possession of herself, she tucked her bottom lip out like a child.

"Don't be a drama queen, Hana. It's not like I was about to slit your throat."

The threads of me were already frayed from a harshly interrupted sleep. Her words were a full pair of scissors to them. "Oh, that's it. That's fucking it." I didn't miss the flicker of momentary fear in her eyes, but it was gone as soon as I marched away from her. Her feet scrambled and hit the floor, running after me.

"Where are you *going*?"

I turned on all the lights of every room I moved through, my palm slapping on the switches like doing so would save me from her eeriness. Knocks on wood, right? I slammed my hand against every door I passed. One by one, sleep-tousled heads peered out from the dim of lamp-lit rooms. Everyone was confused and disgruntled by my loudness. Esme was trailing after me now in wide-eyed helplessness.

"You've gone mad," she said weakly. I walked stiffly into the area where we'd been playing board games earlier and, for some reason, everyone followed me without a word. It was like, briefly, I had taken over Esme's mantle.

By that time, my chest had fully started to ache, though I suppose it wasn't all physical. I just knew, deep down to my bone, that something was really, *really* wrong — and the moment I saw Elsa creep in, I felt like a rotten hypocrite for convincing her not to tell the others what had happened.

"We need to talk," I said to the room at large.

Alice

I came in behind Elsa. I honestly don't know if she particularly liked me, seeing as one of her first impressions of me was, well, a bit *knife*-y, but I found comfort in her. She was predictably nihilistic and was the most opposite person to my sister I could think of. The more she wanted to be alone, the more I admired her for it and, I think, frustratingly, the more I haunted her like a ghost. She politely tolerated me, and she politely allowed me to peer around her like her own personal shih tzu. When Hana saw me, I saw a flush of shame enter her expression. What about? Our conversation earlier?

"We need to talk," she said, having difficulty looking at both me and Elsa. That was fine, because she could glower at the boys, who'd nobly brought up the vanguard like they were game to fix whatever was going on. Esme, unlike herself, had pushed herself practically up against the wall. She was still wearing her dumb heart print pyjamas. They made her look like an oversized five-year-old. "It's about something that happened a couple of days ago —"

"Couldn't it have waited until breakfast?" Cannon drawled. The bags under his eyes had gotten worse. I guess he found it hard to sleep after Esme humiliated him in front of everyone.

"No. Not really. Kind of can't get back to sleep."

"Now that's all of us," Elsa said, not out of bitterness, but pure wistful melancholy. She was such a light sleeper. Esme was looking between all of us in mute appeal. Her eyes caught mine and I swear she was trying to communicate, but fuck, I can't read minds. Hana breathed in deeply. She was rapidly and aggressively massaging her chest like her heart had stopped or something.

"Alice?" she directed to me. "Can I tell them?"

Because I hadn't fully woken up yet, there was a blank space of white noise after she asked. I scrambled to think of what she was talking about. Then, slowly, as everyone's eyes turned on me, the horror that had been dogging me for the past two days returned to me as its rightful queen. I swallowed.

"Alice?" Finn asked. He'd been so nice to me earlier, but he was looking at me now with the same kind eyes as before. I wondered if he was going to look at me again like that. Oh god, once everyone knew, were they going to drive me straight to a police station? How would it work? I'm an English citizen in Sweden. Would they have to call up my dad? Oh god, I was going to disappoint my dad. I licked my lips. My dad would be proudest of me if I owned up to what I'd done wrong. He'd be *more* ashamed of me if I stood there begging Hana to keep my dirty, murderous secret. I was sorry for it, too. I wish I'd never done it.

"Go on," I whispered. Actually, it was more of a croak. I instantly looked at the floor, hoping for an immediate interpolation on everything I'd done wrong, how this vacation was fucked, and how we should all call it quits. Hana took some time to gather her own courage, though. It was weird. *She* had nothing to be ashamed of.

"Something's going on with Esme," she started. It was probably the most mystical start she could have come up with. Nobody knew what to say, and Esme immediately jumped on the defence.

"How am *I* the problem, suddenly? *She's* the one who pulled a knife on me!"

"What?" Finn said.

Cannon's hands had frozen on each side of his face in the process of rubbing the tiredness out of his eyes. Elsa was stock-still in front of me; I couldn't read anything from the tension in her shoulders. She was always a bit tense, after all.

"*Pulled a knife?* What are you on about?"

"Alice pulled a knife on me," Esme declared defiantly, pushing her chin out. Her eyes flashed as she looked towards me. "She went for my throat and —"

"And I saw her slit it," Hana said. She was scrutinising the floor. "I saw her kill you." Everyone stopped talking for a moment. Pure, uncut silence. I hadn't realised how tightly I was holding my hands together, like I was pressing my guilt between two sticky palms. They say you can staunch the bleeding with pressure, but can you staunch the loathing, too? Little white lights were flickering in front of my eyes. I saw her kill you — *I saw her kill you* —

I saw her kill you.

"Well," Esme said. "Cat's out of the bag." Her anger and stubbornness had vanished. She didn't even really look like my sister. More a ceramic doll of her. One of those figures at a wax museum. Elsa shifted, and I was exposed to the eye-line of everyone in the room. I was sweating and shivering at the same time.

"I saw her in the bathroom." Elsa hugged herself. She was wearing another one of her cardigans — a striped thing cropped short above her waist. "She was bleeding pretty bad, but she wasn't dead."

"No. And she didn't have a mark on her either, did she?" Hana chewed on the inside of her cheek as she spoke. "Nothing that would give out that much blood. Almost like…"

"Like what?" Cannon challenged. "Like she healed super fast? Like she's Wolverine?"

"I'm being serious."

"It don't *sound* serious."

"She's right," I said. It came out in a squeak, but they all looked at me again like it was a discordant note. I swallowed. "I was right there. I cut her throat. I remember how it felt when the knife went through her skin, the meat of it, the… I didn't imagine it. She fell to the floor. The blood got everywhere."

"We saw the blood," Finn reminded Cannon. His face was losing some of its healthy pallor. "We thought it looked like a murder scene."

"Can we take a moment to appreciate what she just said?" Esme snapped.

"Pure psycho murderer poetry."

"I regret it!" I announced, my voice wavering even more. I wouldn't believe myself, either. "I wish I hadn't done it, okay? I don't even know why I did, I... just got so *angry*."

"I can believe that." Elsa said it so quietly, I wasn't sure if anyone else heard. Esme's bright eyes turned from me to her, then back again. Something in her jaw twitched.

"Oh, I'm sorry. Does everybody want to take turns sticking the knife in my throat? Elsa, are you going to go first?" She paused, then laughed. It wasn't a mirthful sound. "Is that why you asked if you should all stand in line? You were talking about *murdering me*, weren't you?" Elsa's arms tightened around her slight frame. I swear I could hear her teeth grind. "Anyone else going to, I don't know, mourn me? Is Hana the only one who fucking cares?"

The room was feeling increasingly like a vacuum. Everybody was refusing to look at each other, and most of all they were refusing to look at Esme. Kaida, short and endearing in her white night gown, looked almost ashamed when she tentatively said, "I care." I think it was the fact that she was the only one who said anything, which, somehow, made it sound so insincere. Esme's shoulders heaved up. For a moment, she might even have looked heartbroken.

"I mean..." Byron finally said, hugging the corner of the room away from everyone else. "She's clearly not dead, is she? I think maybe it's all been a misunderstanding?" He looked around for confirmation. Finn latched on second, bobbing his head up and down. His colour hadn't returned to him, but he was trying.

"Which we should be glad for. And maybe it's not the right time to be doing this whole cabin thing?"

There were soft murmurs of agreement. Hana was standing stock-still with her back to the dining table, which had been pushed to one side to clear space on the floor. Her fingers were white with pressure, wrapped around her elbow. There was a burst of sudden laughter from Esme, which sounded more like a hound's bark, and bit at me just as sharp.

"I'm not cutting my holiday short just because you're all self-centred freaks. By all means, *leave* if you want. At least then I'll know for sure which of you are fakes and which of you aren't."

"Esme," Cannon said quietly. "That ain't fair —"

"Maybe it's definitely for the best for you, Cannon. They don't do rehab out in the woods, remember?"

"And you wonder why none of us are mourning you," Elsa snapped. "You wonder why Alice got so fucking — *pissed* — at you."

"Let it all out, Elsa. God knows it's been a while since you really let your *inhibitions* get the better of you."

"Enough!" Finn rarely raised his voice, so thankfully, all at once, everybody shut up. His eyes were wide and anxious. "This isn't the best time to talk about all this. Let's regroup in the morning, yeah? Hana? Is that all right?"

"Like I said, I don't think I'll be able to get back to sleep."

"Well, try anyway," Finn appealed desperately. "Please."

Despite his appeal, none of us moved. I felt light on my feet, like I was floating; like none of it was real. I wished I had never come here with them. I wished, and I rarely ever wished this, that I was still at home. At least that was predictable. At least I had learned how to compartmentalise that. The most unsettling part was that I felt like I didn't recognise her, my own sister. I felt like I was looking at a startlingly clear reflection of her — too pristine, even. *Her freckles*, I realised. All her freckles across the bridge of her nose, and some on her brow, were missing. What a stupid detail to focus on. But then again, maybe I'd have gone mad if I didn't.

"Well," Cannon finally said, stretching his arms out above his head. "I'm too tired for this. I'll see y'all in the morning." He turned from us. Byron trailed after him, then quiet and miserable Kaida. Hana, Finn, Elsa, Esme and I, we all stood still in the wake of their departure. Finn backed out once he realised none of us were leaving first. Then Elsa, with a quick and bitter turn of her heel. Esme's lips were pressed tightly together, like if she pried them open again, she'd let out a sound she didn't like.

"Go to sleep, Alice," Hana finally said. "I'm sorry I woke you all up."

Esme

I can't get the way Hana looked at me out of my head — like I was already rotting. Something putrid that had settled at the top of her stomach. Why had everything changed so much and so suddenly? It was Alice's fault. Alice had tried to kill me. Why did it feel like everyone blamed me for it? Hana slept in the dining area, having collected cushions and a throw blanket from one of the sofas and pushed them up against the cabin windows. I remained alone in the four-poster bed we'd shared, trying to remember how this whole incident had started. I'd come to at the end of the bed, crouching, trying to hide my eyes from the light, and she'd looked at me like embalming fluid was leaking out of my lungs.

I wish I could get all this thought of *death* out of me. I never used to think about death at all. Why should I? I was still young and fresh and a college queen. Death was reserved for distant mothers and old aunts I had never met; strangers who made headlines; nightmare stories from hushed roommates. There was no reason for that five-letter word to *ever* be a part of my vocabulary otherwise. But after Alice tried to kill me, it felt like I was always considering *death* as a lingering part of my identity. Like, I would pause and wonder if my skin smelled too sweet or if I still had feeling in my toes.

I didn't sleep at all that night. I remember that I couldn't — that I wouldn't — and I know that I wasn't dreaming anything because of that. At some point in the early morning hours, I heard what sounded like a distant humming coming from outside the window. I thought it was some kind of natural phenomena — I don't know, something easily explained. I was too absorbed in self-pity to want to find another explanation for it. It was only when the humming grew louder that it came to the forefront of my mind. It sounded like a child who was contemplating whether or not they should start bawling — the warning whines of a toddler about to throw a tantrum. I swung my legs off the side of the bed, and they suddenly felt so heavy. I'd been having trouble with waking up and not being able to move my body for a little while. I thought it was sleep paralysis, but this felt… different.

The crying was pounding in my ears. It sounded like it was right in the room with me, which couldn't be possible. I turned my head, and I spotted the shape of it crawling along the wall where its frame met the ceiling. My stomach lurched. The bottoms of my feet tingled. Any other day, I would have *screamed* bloody murder until someone, anyone, came into the room with me. I always told myself that if I ever saw a ghost or something, that would be the first thing I'd do — just so no one could call me crazy. They'd have seen it, too, you know? But in that moment, I thought if I called for any one of my friends, it would be like admitting defeat. They had already shown their true colours. Why should I scream for them now?

It glistened like an oil slick as it descended from the shadows, a miasma of spewing scales. A tapering head led the way of its descent, and the tip of a forked tongue brushed up against the top of the room's dresser. When it opened its mouth, I heard that keening, awful cry again, and I couldn't breathe. It was in the room with me. It was approaching me. It was coming for me. My hands wouldn't move, and my legs had gone numb. I could only sit there and welcome it — watch it slide like velvet over the brushed wooden surfaces. When its mouth stopped in front of my face, I saw what it was.

A snake.

Its eyes were invisible amidst its wet scales, but I could feel it analysing me. I finally managed to pry my lips apart, my pride going out through the cracked open window that whispered in the cool breeze of a summer dawn. Before the smallest sound could escape me, the snake lurched forward.

It pushed into my throat, that slick serpent head. I choked, grasped at my throat, but it pushed and it pushed no matter how I resisted. It tasted like gasoline and blood, and between the child's cries, I swear I could hear it grunting, growling. I keeled back on the bed, and it followed me. I thrashed and kicked, but nothing would eject it out of my system. Tears coursed down my cheeks. I stared at the slanted ceiling, it descending lower and closer over my head like it was watching me, too; soothing me as I took in the bile of this child-mimicking monster. When its tail had slipped between my teeth, I could feel it settle in my gut. I balked and gagged, wanting nothing more than to vomit it out with the rest of the life that remained in me. I would stick my fingers down my throat if I had to. I would do anything.

It's just a nightmare. Sweet child, you're only dreaming. My uncle would come into my bedroom at night when I had those awful dreams. He would sit on the edge of the mattress and pat my thigh, repeating over and over that I was only dreaming. I was only dreaming.

I had been dreaming for days. This was only a nightmare.

I would wake up soon.

Hana

I woke up first from more restless dreams of girls chasing me through woods, them all resembling Esme, so I forced myself to atone for the confusion of the previous night by preparing the first meal of the day. I whipped up some scrambled eggs with cuts of ham and salami, and a little broccoli for green. The methodical routine of cracking one egg after the other was comforting in its mind-numbing ease. It gave me all the time in the world to picture my girlfriend trying to cave my chest in with her whole weight. I went over that memory with a fine-toothed comb, making sure I hadn't overreacted — making sure I'd been sensible about the whole thing. I've got to say, I think I was pretty level-headed for how creepy the entire interaction had been.

The denizens of the three different bedrooms drifted into the kitchen with solemn slowness. Finn tried to make light talk about how good the eggs smelled, but all I could do was mutely hand him a plate with some ketchup and shredded cheese. The three boys silently forked the mostly yellow mix into their mouths as they crowded around the kitchen island, and the girls sat on the sofa where I'd slept the remainder of the morning away, their knees all identically curled up as they pushed the eggs backwards and forwards, backwards and forwards. My mother had raised me to be very particular about leaving a clean plate, so, even if I was the only person I'd disappoint in that room, I nobly finished off my own breakfast with a spotlessness that would have made her proud.

Esme came in when the eggs were cold. She had changed into a little red dress fit for the sunniest summer, dotted with tiny white flowers and finished off with a dainty bow at her sternum. Her face was healthy and blushed, her lashes dark and spidery. She looked nothing like the girl who had been sulking in her bed for two days in a row. I couldn't help but stare at her as she walked past me, wafting a heady scent of tuberose and jasmine. She scooped up her plate like it was freshly made and got to finishing off the whole affair as cleanly as I'd done. When she finally noticed we were all looking at her, she raised her brows and cleared her mouth.

"What? Have I got something on my face?"

The boys looked at each other, searching for the correct answer. The girls kept staring. I was also in the staring camp. Esme directed her blue gaze to me and slowly set down her plate. "Ha-*na*?" she lilted, like she was coaxing a toddler into telling her the truth. I felt my cheeks burn despite myself.

"You look nice," I said, dumbly. Very, very dumbly. She smiled, puzzled.

"I look nice every day. No need to stare."

But there was something more to it. Something almost... *uncannily* perfect. She looked airbrushed in person. I couldn't wrap my head around it. I looked for a hint of her freckles beneath the thin veil of concealer, but her skin was flawless. She looked like she was made of wax.

"You're all right after last night, then?" Finn asked gently. He watched her warily, like he wasn't quite sure she was real either. Esme tilted her head, her smile unwavering, her eyes bright and unblinking.

"Why wouldn't I be?"

We didn't know what to say to that. Maybe if we explained, we'd be poking the bear. I don't think any of us had the energy to deal with another quarrel. Esme set down her plate, still waiting, and let the quiet settle all through the room with an eerie stillness. Byron cleared his throat.

"Well, it's all good then, yeah?" he offered. He looked between all of us. "Bygones and all that?"

"Whatever do you mean?" Esme asked sweetly. She let a hand drape over the edge of the kitchen island and, instinctively, Byron jerked his elbow away. "You all seem awfully on edge."

"So did you," Cannon drawled slowly, "last night."

Whatever invisible dam we had put up to fend off the bear was slowly coming down out of confusion. The girls had unfurled their legs on the sofa. Kaida stood up and approached Esme with a look of wide-eyed concern, like she'd shown up in a hospital gown instead of her pretty summer dress. She reached out the hand that wasn't balancing her plate of eggs and set it down on top of Esme's on the island.

"You know we all care about you?" she insisted. "Right?" It was well-intentioned, like a positive quote that would be passed around on social media. Esme stared at her, her smile fixed in place. I was getting a crawling sensation up my spine. Instincts that I'd inherited from my primitive ancestors were screaming in me. When man first met his predator, it had frightened him enough to pass a chill down the spine through all generations to come. It must have been a really good lesson, if it stuck for so long.

"Why would I ever doubt that?" Esme asked, tilting her head, smiling patronisingly at Kaida. Their fingers interlinked, pink skin pinching white between each other's knuckles. Kaida's mouth broke into a relieved grin that creased her brown eyes prettily. She had such a nice smile. She was, I think, a genuinely nice girl. "You're the best friends a girl could have. I know all your secrets and you know all of mine. Right?" She looked around at the rest of us. I saw Kaida relax and start to pull her hand away, but then stop with a little confused frown. "You've all been so sweet. You've never hidden anything from me. I'm sorry I told everyone about your rehab, Cannon — that was so personal, and really, I was *privileged* that you ever told me any of that."

"I didn't, though," Cannon said, his own brow creasing. "I mean, you didn't know about it because I *told* you —"

"And I was so unfair to you, Elsa," Esme continued. "You're right. You've all a right to be so angry with me. After all, if I weren't around, there'd be no one else who knew you for what you truly are."

Kaida was really pulling at her own hand now, but Esme wasn't letting her go. The smile had vanished from her face.

"Esme," I said, but she held up her other hand. I was ashamed that I immediately fell silent.

"Wouldn't it have just been perfect if Alice really *had* killed me? So many secrets would have died with me. That's why none of you are particularly bothered, right? I'm an *inconvenience*."

"Esme," Finn pleaded now. "You know that's not true, yeah? That's not what any of us have said."

"But it's what you're all thinking. You aren't really my friends, are you? You're just scared of me."

"Please let go of my hand," Kaida said in a small voice. She looked like she was in a lot of pain, her eyes bright and watery. "I'm your friend."

"No, Kaida." There was a flash of too-white teeth. "You're just great to have around because your daddy wants to fuck me so much, he funds our summer holiday."

There was a sound of a sickly, gristly *snap*. Kaida cried out in pain, her knees buckling as her hand remained in Esme's at an odd, contorted angle. Suddenly everyone was on their feet. The room started to spin.

"What the fuck," I said, and instinctively reached behind me for the little knife I'd used to cut the ham and salami. The silver sheen was still sticky with the spiced meat juices. Finn pried at Kaida's hand while at the same time trying to soothe Esme. Cannon looked like he was fight or flight. Byron caught my eye, saw me holding the knife, and very imperceptibly nodded.

"You've gone crazy," Elsa said from across the room. She was holding Alice behind her, whose eyes were wide as the little cups in the kitchen cabinet.

Esme's teeth were so white and long. The way her jaw fit under her skin was unfamiliar. I'd memorised the side of her face over two months, falling more and more in love with it. I started to circle behind her, my palm wet with sweat.

"I feel great," Esme said. "We're going to have so much fun." The force with which she lurched toward Kaida rocked Finn backward. I think that's what spared him from getting hurt in the collateral. My girlfriend's big, perfect teeth landed on Kaida's neck, and I flawlessly memorised the expression of shock and agony on her face before her throat exploded in a sudden rush of blood and skin. The room erupted in one long, terrified scream. I could only act out of instinct, launching myself at Esme's back, digging the small, sticky knife into her shoulder. It distracted her enough to pull back. Her lips were deep crimson and fresh blood dribbled down her chin.

The second sound was the cold shatter of Byron breaking an egg-y plate over her head. I ducked when the shards flew my way. In the midst of that, Cannon jumped forward and pulled Kaida out of Esme's grasp. It was a flurry of bodies with my girlfriend at the centre of them all, a cringing, bloody figure in her little red dress. I hadn't pulled the knife back out. If she turned on me, I was unarmed.

"Don't just fucking stand there!" Elsa yelled. "Get away from her!" I snapped to and scuttled backward, picking up a fork along the way, measuring the circumstance of the room toward the nearest door. Cannon and Finn had Kaida between them. She stood dazed and white as one of our blanket sheets, blood pooling on her collarbone. Esme reached around her shoulder and pulled the knife out. On her face was a look of earnest betrayal, as though she'd expected me to cheer her on as she cannibalised one of our friends.

What the *fuck*?

"Esme," Cannon drawled. Kaida's arm kept slipping from around his neck, and he'd somehow got her blood on the front of his comic book t-shirt. It blended into the graphic art reds quite well. "Don't try anything else, all right? We're gonna restrain you if you do." He wasn't talking to her like a normal human being would talk to another when they attempted to tear someone's throat out. He was bargaining with a feral animal. She tilted her head at him, offended that he'd distracted her from the knife in her hand. Slowly, she licked her lips, the wet, glistening tongue dragging over her too big, too perfect teeth.

"Restrain me?" she repeated hollowly, as if it was the dumbest thing she'd ever heard. My back was to the door that led to the hallway with the bathroom and the porch exit. What would I do if I went out that way? Just keep running into the woods? Scream for help and hope the birds heard me? I reoriented my thoughts. There were other cabins out there. I'd seen them when I went out for fresh air. I couldn't speak Swedish, but if I could somehow get Elsa with me —

"Touch me and you're next, Cannon Moody."

"You're not yourself, Esme," Finn said. He was holding onto Kaida's arm tighter the more she slumped. She was going to bleed out if I didn't do something. If I didn't get that help. "This was just another accident, all right? But Kaida needs some help."

"It wasn't an accident," Esme replied blankly. "I meant to do that. I'd do it again, even."

My eyes caught Alice's across the room. She was nodding at me. *Run*, she was telling me. Fuck. The people we'd met in Gothenburg had spoken perfectly fine English. I could do this. I slid my heels backward, cursing when the floorboards creaked beneath my weight.

Esme's head snapped towards me, her nostrils flaring. *The betrayer.* "Going somewhere, Hana?" Her dark eyes swept contemptuously over the fork I was holding up in my hand. I wondered if she was really going to kill me. She liked me, didn't she? Fuck, fuck, *fuck*.

I've never thought much of Cannon Moody, but I'll never forget his impulsive bravery in that moment. He threw himself at her back, wrapping his lean arm around her throat, getting her into a chokehold. I turned and ran as fast as I could. I regretted it the moment my bare feet hit the grass and I felt the wet texture of the dirt. I regretted separating myself from people I wouldn't necessarily call my friends, but who were suddenly my only allies in this isolated woodland. I regretted running at all, because I kept thinking back to my recurring nightmares where I was running across the meadow and the girl that looked like Esme was chasing me, screaming her terrible woodland song. I didn't dare look behind me, just in case that came true. I careened between the trees and felt a stray twig stab into the sole of my foot. Tears of panic and pain sprung to my eyes.

I had never been a daring child. I did as my mother told me. I stood stoically at the edge of the playground while my peers played on the monkey bars. I thought I was better than the reckless athletes. One thing I got into was running — I was a faster runner than anyone my age by the time I turned sixteen. When a friend and I were late for a bus, I was always the one who could run and flag the driver down, waiting the span of sixty seconds for my companion to catch up and go, *Wow, Hana. You should get into marathons.* Running across uneven earth in a forest is different to running down a reasonably maintained street, though. I found myself tripping and stumbling more than I'd ever done in my life. I was yelping out and cursing the air louder than a toddler who'd slid ungracefully off the end of a seesaw. If anyone was following me, I'd be easy to find. I was no stealthy ranger, leaving minimal tracks, soft-footed as the leaves that floated from the canopy overhead. The closeness of the trees blanketed my ragged breaths, more from adrenaline and fear than actual physical exertion. Every inhale brought stale, dying leaves. Every exhale was a sharp jab in my ribs.

Then I broke out through the trees. I wavered on the edge of them, grateful to see a small red cabin greeting me in quiet tranquillity. I took two steps towards it, unable to believe my luck, when its door flung open. Cannon and Finn stumbled through, the blood-soaked form of Kaida held between them. "*Gogogo,*" Cannon was firing at me. I tried to explain that I had, I really had, but they pushed past me. I could hear the unbridled chaos of shouts and scrambling feet behind us as I followed them. Something was whistling nearby — Kaida, struggling to breathe, every attempt a hiss of air through a throat that didn't seem to be working. Finn and Cannon's hands were slippery with her blood.

I got turned about, I told myself, furious. *God, you idiot, you absolute* — and yet the shouts weren't getting any further away. The trees were packed so close together. Underneath it all, the yells and Kaida's death rattles, I could hear a familiar song that made nausea crawl up my spine.

"Stop," I said, but the boys didn't listen. I threw out my hands, catching them by their shoulders. "*Stop!*" They drew up short, heavy in the scent of copper and leaves. We all stared at the cramped space between the trees. The music came nearer, and the shouts and cries, and the pounding feet of living things approaching, assaulting, crowding —

Elsa and Alice collided with us, Byron just behind them holding a broken shard of a plate so tightly in his fist that I could see blood welling up between his fingers. We stared at each other, unable to make a sound besides small whimpers of fear and heavy breaths. We held onto each other, our minds blank. Slowly, slowly the forest settled around us. Without the trampling, the yelling, there was only the wind beneath the trees and that distant, childish hum. That, too, seemed to fade. We listened anyway, paralysed on our feet. We were all afraid to move; to perpetuate the chase.

The light hadn't changed. Nothing seemed to have moved. Regardless, I know it was some time before Byron spoke, his voice tremulous as it broke the pact of silence we had instinctively made with the trees. "Is she dead?"

Kaida's eyes had shut as she dangled between Cannon and Finn like something rotten and crucified. I couldn't bear to look at her.

"She's breathing," Cannon answered. He was hoarse, barely able to get an octave out of the tightness of his throat. His eyes were bloodshot. "I don't know how much longer for."

"Not longer if we don't get her help," Elsa said tightly. She was still holding onto my shoulder. I was grateful that she didn't let go. "We need to. There are other cabins, people with cars —" The cars were all in the same place — our rental, too — in a little park at the edge of the woodlands.

"I tried," I whispered. "I tried, but somehow I ran back to the cabin in a circle."

They all exchanged glances. Byron wet his lips.

"That's like a classic trope, isn't it? You think you're going straight, but you run round in a circle… sorry, what I'm saying is, you get turned about the woods real easy. You might think you didn't —"

I know what he meant to say. I couldn't disagree with him, nor did I want to. I *wanted* to have been incompetent. That meant we still had hope.

"Then don't waste time," Elsa snapped. "We need to go. *Now.*"

The unspoken subject of Esme hung in the air between us. What had happened? What had she become? Why were we cowering from her like she was a wolf, and not like she was a human being gone mad? Something had happened in that cabin which was not tethered to the reality that we lived in. I couldn't explain it beyond anything superficial, but I was convinced that whoever we had left behind was not really, truly Esme, but I couldn't tell you either that she wasn't. To imply that it was someone else would beg the question of where my actual girlfriend had gone. I reflected back on the nightmares I had had. Esme screaming from the line of trees. For help?

No. It was Kaida who needed our help now. I needed to get myself together. I couldn't run a marathon physically, but I could run one mentally. Dissociate for just long enough to get the poor girl some help.

If it was going to be that straightforward.

alice

It should have been simple, finding another cabin. I'd seen them from just outside our porch, one or two meadows away. If we walked through the woods, found the other end instead of circling back around to *our* end... it shouldn't have been that difficult. We practically stared at our feet to make sure we went in a straight line, but it seemed like it was as Byron said: we got turned about without realising and we always came back to the cabin. *Our* cabin. All the while, Kaida was bleeding out. I'd never seen someone bleed out before. My sister didn't count, did she, as she wasn't dead or dying? We tried to pretend for a good while that we'd be able to find our neighbours in the end. That she was going to survive. That we were going to get out.

The fifth time that we came back out in front of our cabin, Cannon yelled and kicked uselessly at the edge of the porch. We didn't know if Esme was inside anymore. If she was, I thought the only good the noise would do was call her out to get us. I swear I saw her silhouette through one of the windows, watching us. What good entertainment we must be making for her. Unlike Hana, I couldn't find myself separating my sister wholly from that... *thing* that assaulted Kaida. It was like I knew it was still her, but she was wearing some sort of veneer, and I was cross at her for not coming out from under it and apologising for being a bitch again. You know, in the end, she *did* always apologise to me. That made it seem worse again that I'd tried to stab her. Maybe I'd been wearing a veneer in that moment, too — or maybe pretending that I wasn't myself was me wearing a veneer afterwards. It was all hard to unravel inside of my head.

It didn't help that the woods made my mind fuzzy. The pungent scent of damp greenery, of something very *old*, rotted inside of my throat and up through my sinuses. The air was so thick I thought I would gag on it, and that reflex followed me with each step. So, on that fifth time, I had to crouch down and balance myself on the ground — hang my head between my knees like my dad had always coached me to do when I got queasy. None of it helped, though the air was a little clearer once we were out of the trees. I squeezed my eyes shut, and I think I still saw the leaves crunching underfoot.

"This is ridiculous," Elsa declared, but there was a note of desperation beneath her bad temper. "We can't be getting turned about every single time."

"What's the other explanation?" Byron countered nervously. He looked too small in a striped crochet shirt he must have picked up from some vintage market. His skin was prickling with chill beneath the flapping sleeves. "The woods are moving as we walk through them? You've got to — I mean, that sounds *more* ridiculous."

"Is it, though?" Hana asked wearily. "Sure, maybe once is us getting turned about, but every single time? We're not going far enough to get so lost. If we were, we wouldn't keep finding our way back *here*."

"Plus, something's off about this whole thing." Finn was duly holding onto Kaida as Cannon marched about the perimeter of the cabin. His eyes were like two black holes inside of his face; like he'd seen too much. "It wouldn't be the strangest thing yet for the trees to be moving."

"That's a stretch," Byron argued. "That's pure fantasy at this point."

"Okay, does it matter?" Hana broke in again. "She's losing blood. We've bigger things to worry about than if trees move."

"But that's why we're worrying about it! We need to get her to a hospital —"

I looked up at the window again. There was a girl behind the glass, but I couldn't tell if she had my sister's face. Her palm pressed up against the frame, almost wistful. "We can't stay here," I said. "I think she's still inside."

"Inside is where we can help Kaida the most," Elsa snapped. "There's a first aid kit in the bathroom. Esme is so small. We'll knock her out and tie her up or something."

"Yeah, you gonna try?" Cannon had finally circled back around to us. His face was taut and menacing. "Because if I couldn't hold her down, I wish you good luck."

"You didn't want to hurt her. I know you still have —"

"What? You think I care about that *thing* in there? Whoever you think she is, Elsa, that's not Esme. That girl's not even human."

"Okay," Byron muttered, "now we're going off the deep end."

"I kind of know what he means." Hana looked like she hated admitting it. "She just — I don't know, she looks like someone drew her from memory or something. It's Esme, but it's *not*."

Elsa bit down on her lip and her tongue. She couldn't argue. None of us could, unless we were totally delusional and in denial. Normal Esme wouldn't have been able to tear someone's throat out like she'd done, straight for the jugular without any hesitation. Normal Esme thought violence was brutish and overrated. Byron waved his hands uselessly, then looked down at his feet. I breathed in deeply and repeated, "We *can't* stay here."

"If we go back into the woods," Hana said, "we're just going to find our way back here again."

"Then we don't try to leave the woods," Cannon declared. "If she wants to keep leading us back here, that means she don't want us out there. So, we'll stay there. She can come find us if she's so desperate."

"Are you mad?" Elsa pointed sharply at Kaida. "If we go back into the woods and do *nothing*, she *will* die."

We all fell quiet at that. What was a grisly accident was slowly revealing itself as a drawn-out murder. We had no way to really help Kaida, even with the first aid kit inside. She'd already lost so much blood, and if it wasn't the blood, she was so shocked that — even when she *was* conscious — she had been mute for however long we'd trekked through the forest. Kaida was going to die, and we were all going to watch her bite the bullet.

"We've no choice," Cannon said without looking her in the eye. "If we stay, we'll all die."

It sounded so ridiculous to say it; to talk about Esme like she was a monster. I found myself getting to my feet anyway, following them back to the edge of the woods. I looked over my shoulder one last time, not sure what I was hoping to see. The girl was gone from the window, if she had ever really been there at all.

Hana

I ended up watching over Kaida for the night. I told myself everyone else was too exhausted, but they slept with their backs to her like they couldn't bear to watch her die. Could I blame them? Not really. Maybe I'd've done the same if I wasn't the last one awake. We didn't have camping gear. Why would we? We thought we'd be spending our summer in a little red cabin in the picturesque Swedish countryside. I sat with my arse on the bare ground, holding the hand of a girl I'd barely known these past two months. I was fascinated by how utterly washed of colour she was. Her palm was ice-cold against mine, and her eyes were as bright as the stars that I couldn't see from under the trees. Uselessly, we'd all checked our phones for a signal out there, but of course there wasn't any. I thought if I could just give it one more try, I'd find another cabin. Instinctively, though, I knew I wouldn't.

"If my dad was here," Kaida gurgled, "he would know... he would know how to fix this." It was the first time she had really spoken since the whole incident. I stared at her, not sure how to answer. "He is a very. Fixing man."

With her life passing before her eyes, Kaida's cultivated English slipped. I could hear the Japanese in the way she let the syllables slur. A stone formed in my throat and my eyes started to sting. I wished I hadn't been the last one awake.

"Is your father like that?" she continued. "A very hard man?"

"No," I said. "He's a very sleazy man. He left my mum because she didn't live up to his idea of a traditional wife."

"Oh," she whispered. "I'm sorry."

"Don't be. My mum's strong. If she was here, I think she'd know how to fix everything, too. She always does."

"Yes. My *papa*, too." Kaida swallowed thickly. "He always really liked Esme. He said she was a very pretty girl." My skin crawled uncomfortably at that. That's not exactly what you want your father to say about one of your friends. "If he knew this was happening, he would try to find help — for me, but also for her."

"I think you'd be a lot more important to him right now, Kaida."

"I hope so, Hana. But he really, really liked Esme."

How much? I would have asked at any other time. Maybe our fathers were alike after all, in the worst of ways. I squeezed her hand tighter. "Do me a favour, and don't die on me. Not right now. Okay?"

"Okay." She agreed bravely, but I know she had no way to adhere to the promise. In the small hours of the night, while I was slipping from consciousness to unconsciousness, passing between dreams of girls peering at me between trees and snakes twining through the branches, she passed while still holding my hand. I wish I'd gotten to know her better. She deserved more than just to be remembered as Esme's friend.

I came to cramped and cold, and I realised they were all watching me, holding the hand of a dead girl. Anger surged in me, then grief, then numbness. I let her white, unyielding fingers go.

"Fuck," Byron said, like it had sunk in at last that it was real — all of it. Him and the rest of them were getting some fine bags under their eyes, which made me realise I probably wasn't the last one awake at all. I could still feel the chill of Kaida's hand in mine, no matter how much I wiped my fingers on the fabric of my trousers. "She's dead. She's actually dead."

"What did you think would happen?" Elsa asked flatly. She hugged her knees, staring at Kaida's body as though she couldn't quite reconcile with herself whether it was real or not. Dirt was smudged across her cheek. Cannon got to his feet and approached me and the dead girl, gesturing for me to move away from her.

"What're you going to do?" It was a dumb question for me to ask, like I was defensive over this last memory of her. His mouth twitched, a small spasm at the corner of his lips.

"I'm not going to leave her exposed to the animals, am I?"

God, we hadn't even thought of that, the local wildlife. We were so busy trying to escape the human in the cabin, we hadn't paused to think if we were actually safe out in the woods. If maybe there were other things that wanted to feast on us as well. My stomach churned, and I stood up to help him. Alice came forward, too. Her hair was limp and greasy down her shoulders. "Now you care about leaving bodies lying around?" Cannon drawled, turning a hostile stare toward her. She flinched, and the few steps she had taken, she began to rescind.

"That's harsh," I defended her. "You know she didn't mean to do it."

"Do I? Do *you*? All I know is this mess started when she drew a knife on her own sister. I'd like her to stay far away from me in the meantime."

A little chill crawled over my skin. Really? In-fighting? Last I checked, yes, Alice had tried to kill her own sister, but we'd all tried to do the same thing yesterday. You know, after she ripped Kaida's throat out with her own fucking teeth.

"It's okay, Hana," Alice said awkwardly. "I wouldn't trust me either." Her futile attempt to reassure me seemed to incense Cannon further. He barked out a mocking, choked laugh.

"You Martin girls are a special breed, y'know that? Kind of breed they ought to put out back."

"Cannon," Finn warned. He wouldn't even look at Alice, though. Not anymore.

"I'm only saying what we're all thinking. There's something wrong with you two. Something rotten in that household. And it was a mistake to ever come out here with the both of you."

I couldn't disagree with him, but I smarted for Alice. I might have only been twenty then, but it felt like a chasm between that and when I was seventeen years old. Her smallness in comparison to the rest of us made her seem even more like a kid. Besides, a part of me wished she'd gotten it right that night and slit Esme's throat for real. Maybe Kaida would still be alive, then, even if my girlfriend wasn't. I didn't even know if my girlfriend as I knew her was still with us, really.

We buried Kaida haphazardly. We didn't have any shovels, only our hands, so we didn't go particularly deep; just enough to brush some soil over her. Byron watched us sceptically, notably not helping. "That won't be deep enough to keep the animals away, will it?" he observed, and I saw the corner of Cannon's mouth twitch again. I had a feeling this guy was a minute hand away from unpleasantly exploding on somebody.

"It's better than nothing."

We stood and looked at the sad little mound we had left behind. I had an inkling Kaida would have preferred to be buried anywhere else. Maybe if we found someone and got back to civilisation, I'd ask them to come back and dig her up again. Take her back home where her father would know what to do. Cannon cleared his throat with authority, disrupting my thoughts.

"Much as I don't want to go back to the cabin, we can't stay out here forever. There's no reliable food, no reliable water… we have to keep trying to reach someone else. Ask for help." I realised he was taking the lead on things, and it perplexed me more than it made me admire him. We'd just laid to rest one of his closest friends and he was tackling this like we were on *The Walking Dead*. I didn't want anyone to be a hero. I just wanted to get out of there and go home. "There's a thing folks do when they know they'll get turned about in the woods, see. They mark the trees they've passed by, that way they know when they're doubling back and when they're treading new dirt. I'll tear up my shirt if I have to, but I've only got so much of it. Just thin strips'll do. We can tie them round the trunks."

We murmured a sort of begrudging agreement. I wondered if I was biased against him because of what Elsa had implied yesterday. Maybe I was reading too much into it, but it sounded like she thought he had feelings for Esme. I'd had an inkling that maybe they'd messed around in the past, but I'd never thought it was something so serious on either end. It would be stupid of me to hold a previous relationship with my girlfriend against someone — the very same girlfriend I'd been wishing had died the very first night we were there. I've done stupider things, though.

Cannon approached the base of the tree that we'd superficially buried Kaida under. He tore the bottom strip off his Venom T-shirt, tying it around the trunk with a grunt. It was sombre and fitting enough — it was just the black edge of it, an appropriate funerary ribbon for our friend.

"Now," he said, turning round to face us. He set his jaw and stared us down with his un-rested dark circles. "Which direction, folks?"

Esme

I'm still me, underneath it all. Under the skin that feels too tight and pristine on my bones, or the teeth that don't seem to fit in my mouth. I'm still me under the taste of blood I can't help but crave; under the music of the woods that I can't seem to escape. And I was still me on that day I killed Kaida. I was fully awake and conscious inside of my own body. I tasted her life on my tongue. It was hot and sweaty, and I could gag just remembering it, but I revel in it, too. It was a successful hunt. It was *such* a powerful feeling.

And I grieved. Kaida was one of the first friends I made at college. She instilled the confidence in me that would prove to be my downfall. This sweet, optimistic girl looked at me and tossed daddy's money on me like we were actual sisters, born and brought up in the same household. I loved that, truly, after hating everything about my own childhood, and resenting everything about my own sister. I thought she was the best friend I could ever have, and I was so excited to meet the rest of her family, hoping they would adopt me in the same way she seemed to have done. I wanted to recreate that innocence that I'd never had in mine. I pictured a doting father figure, and a mother figure I could whisper all my secrets and fears to without visiting a gravestone.

A part of me — and maybe this is dramatic — but a part of me died on the day that I *did* meet her family. The distracted mother was more elusive than a dead one, and the father leered at me across their dining room table like I was the whole fish his wife had brought home from the Asian market. When we stood up to gather the dishes, he brushed up against me, and I could smell decades of cigarettes and alcohol in the linen of his shirt. I would have never seen Kaida again, except when I was leaving, her father came up to me with a larger wad of cash than I'd ever seen in my life. *For being such a pretty guest*, he said. Not a nice one, a polite one, even one who was a good conversationalist — but for being *pretty*. What hurt the most is that Kaida saw it all happen. She saw it all happen, and she walked me down her driveway, grabbed my hand in hers, and said, "Did you like them?" A question as innocent as the rest of her.

She had no right to act so innocent.

That's why I snapped. She came up to me and gushed about how she was still my friend, and I fucking hated her for it. I fucking hated how she burnished everything with the sheen of a giggly, happy-go-lucky schoolgirl. She knew better. She knew better and she never empathised — she just made me feel guilty for not being as accepting of things as she was. How could she ever look me in the face after what her father had done to me? How could she ever look at her *father*?

It was all a nightmare, anyway. Don't tell me you've never lashed out at someone you hated in your nightmares before, knowing you could get away with it. I was in the middle of a nightmare, and I couldn't wake up. I saw her face and I hated it. I hated it, I hated it.

And then I hated myself for hurting her.

I watched them take off into the woods, my friends and my girlfriend, with the same disconnect that I would have with any other dream. The consequences were muffled behind a pane of glass. I stepped out into the garden after them, one, two, and looked up at the trees and realised I had come home at last. This is where I belonged. The woods had been calling to me from the moment I'd arrived at the cabin. Its song, which had once seemed nauseating, even *uninviting*, was now a siren call. It filled me with joy; ecstasy at the thought of running through the trees unleashed, filling the emptiness of my stomach until, at last, I could rest again, sated. If I tilted my head back just enough and breathed in deeply, I could smell the musk of their fear beneath the pungent scents of summer. I felt sweet lucidity and, following that, *power*.

I glanced back at the cabin and saw the shape of the girl I had been watching me from one of the windows. Her mouth worked and worked, begging me to stop, to come back to her, but it was too late. I was a separate being now. I was her, and I was not. She was simply my springboard. My stomach clenched around its disappointing lack of fullness. I had tasted Kaida's blood, but I hadn't feasted on her. If she had to die in this reality, then I should at least honour her with a full consumption. She would come to a stop at some point and, though her flesh would be cold by then, I would pay her the respects due the sweetness of her meat.

Hana

To Cannon's credit, the tying shirts around the trees thing was working. We weren't stumbling back out in front of the cabin like we were being spit out by the woods. We walked carefully through the forest, searching for an end to the leafy crunch underfoot, hoping against hope that we'd find another cabin to get help — but also to have a hearty meal and maybe some good, cold water. My stomach was subsisting only on yesterday's breakfast, and even that had come out in an anxious bout of diarrhoea behind one of the marked trees, which was a horror all its own. Despite it being summer and quite hot in Sweden, the consistent shade of the trees was making it a little too cool, enough to make the sinews between my knuckles hurt.

By what I thought was maybe late afternoon, we circled back around to the first tree we had marked with the bottom strip of Cannon's shirt. Our spirits, minuscule as they were, dilapidated some more. It was better progress than before, but in the end, we'd still gone around in a big circle. Cannon reared himself up with a bravery he didn't feel and said, "Well, we just gotta pick another direction. Mark all the trees in this forest if we have to. There's got to be an end to it." He looked a little silly, his t-shirt slowly turning into a crop top. I looked listlessly around the roots of the tree and then stopped and frowned. The shallow mound where we had buried Kaida had already been disturbed. I tried not to look too hard in case one of her grey-tinged limbs was poking out.

"Suppose we try the cabin again?" Byron asked tentatively. "Just to get some food, you know? We don't want to starve out here."

"You're welcome to," Cannon said in a voice that warned against such a notion. "Try to scream real loud, though, if Esme gets her hands on you." The colour leeched out of Byron's face, and he ducked his head.

"He *is* right," Elsa spoke flatly. Her cardigan had snagged several times on the passing branches and now was wearing more holes than sleeves. "Esme might try us at the cabin, but if we're stubborn, we'll die out here, too."

"You think I'm being stubborn?" Cannon snapped. "Trying to stay alive is *stubborn?*"

"You're doing the best you can," Finn appeased. If there's one thing I'd learned after spending a whole day walking with this group, it was that Finn was always going to try and appease Cannon. It was a little sickening.

"How big are the woods, Elsa?" Alice asked. She had been trailing near the rear of the group, not wanting to catch Cannon's ire. He already seemed incensed that she'd spoken up at all. Elsa blinked, seemingly surprised that her knowledge on the locale was being sought out.

"It'll seem a lot bigger than it is, if we keep getting lost — but the meadows are bigger. The trees around here are more of a border between cabins."

It made us look even more incompetent. I inhaled slowly, scratching at the short stub of my ponytail. It itched where it pulled my hair from my scalp. "We've gone around in circles, and we haven't seen anything to eat. Or any water." A fact. Cannon couldn't get mad at me for stating a fact.

"So, you're all in favour of marching back to the murder house, is that what you're saying?" he drawled.

"You act like we're so fucking helpless if we do." The curse word rolled out of Elsa's mouth without a single effect on her marble-y cadence. She crossed her arms over her chest the way she always did, like she was fending off an intruder into the house that was her body. Her hair was full of dark fly-aways, lending her a sort of *witch of the woods* look. "If Esme tries to hurt us again, we defend ourselves. You're cross at Alice for trying to kill her, but maybe she had the right of it." We all stared at her, uncertain. Cannon cocked his head.

"You can't be serious."

"Why not? You're okay with Esme killing Kaida, but draw the line at us fighting back?"

He sucked in his lips. When the quiet thickened, I said, "You mean — you're saying let's murk Esme?" She wrinkled her nose in confusion, so I hastily added, "*Kill.* You want to *kill* Esme."

"I'm fine with knocking her out." She was so casual about it. I wondered if she'd really hated Esme's guts this whole time. I wondered if they all had. She looked around at the rest of us for confirmation on what we thought. Everyone except for Alice was staring at their feet.

"I think we'd really need to be on our guard," Alice said, her eyes bright and determined. "She moved really fast the last time. And she was *strong*." Elsa nodded. My head swam a little at how factually the two of them were discussing this idea. The words stuttered out of my throat.

"Wait, hold on. Can we not talk about killing my girlfriend so cavalierly? I mean, probably my *ex*-girlfriend after all's said and done, but still."

"*God*, Hana. Are you really so naïve?" Elsa's lip curled. "That girl, whatever she convinced you of, is not who you think she is. I would say she's done worse in her life than threaten to kill someone."

"Hold on," Cannon cut in. "What do you mean by *that*? Murder's a pretty hefty charge." I was going to have to agree with Cannon there. Elsa's eyes flashed, and suddenly her arms uncrossed. It had the same effect as throwing open a door. Or kicking it down. Or setting it on fire.

"Do you think you're the only one she's humiliated with that whole... *rehab* bullshit? She *likes* to dig up dirt; to hold things over people's heads. Do you know why I agreed to come here? She guilted me into it. She implied that — that —" Her mouth sealed up and her cheeks mottled with a patchwork pink colour. We all exchanged glances. Finn, ever the gentle one, was the one to prod.

"She implied what, Elsa?"

Elsa's arms hung limply at her sides and her slender jaw worked and worked and worked over the unsaid words. Her eyes looked feverish in her small face. But then I realised they were glazed with tears.

"My last boyfriend. He took videos of me that I didn't know existed. When we broke up, he, you know..."

"Revenge porn," Cannon intoned, unhelpfully. Her bottom lip screwed up.

"She found them. I don't know how, I mean — she found them before I did. She kept holding them over my head, making me stay sweet to her... I don't know if she downloaded and backed them up or what. I tried to get all of them taken down, but I could never know —" Elsa swallowed.

I was fucking horrified. I couldn't believe Esme had done something so despicable. The Esme I knew would have tongue-lashed the desperate ex who'd break laws just to get back at his girlfriend. I could picture her in my dorm, her head silhouetted against the evening as she blew blunt smoke out through a crack in my window. *Men are fucking disgusting*, she'd say with a dark look in her eye. Not my Esme. No, no, no.

"After what she said to Cannon, I thought she must have something on everyone. How fucked is that? A group of people she's blackmailing all on holiday with her."

We looked around at each other. Byron was white as a sheet. Alice was gnawing on her bottom lip, staring at her shoelaces. Something leaped at the top of my chest.

"Did you know, Alice?" I asked. "Did you know she was blackmailing people?" Silently, she nodded. I pictured her standing in the kitchen again, paralysed with the knife in her hand, blood spattering across her sleeveless turtleneck. "Did she... have something on you?" I regretted asking, just for how sick she looked after. That was all the answer I needed, wasn't it?

"Not... not like revenge porn or anything," she said softly. "I guess it was similarly fucked, though."

"And I didn't tell anyone about my rehab," Cannon said flatly. "I did overdose in her dorm one night, on the pills that she sold me." He looked around at us, making sure we understood what he was implying, before elaborating blankly, "She was my plug."

We fell silent, waiting for someone else to participate in that macabre, voyeuristic reveal. Thankfully, no-one else volunteered anything, including me. I couldn't think of a single thing Esme could have held over my head. The point of blackmail was to make sure the other person knew they were indebted, right? Well, if that was the case, she hadn't done a good job with me. As if reading my mind, Elsa murmured, "You're the exception, aren't you? That's why you like her so much. You haven't been around long enough for her to sink her claws into your dark secrets."

"I didn't know," I said lamely. "I had no idea."

"No." Alice had finally lifted her eyes. "She made sure you didn't. She really liked you, Hana. I don't know if that would have changed, but..." She trailed off, one shoulder shrugging upwards. I know that was supposed to make me feel better in some twisted way. *Hey, your girlfriend's fucked up, but she really did like you!* I put my hands on my knees and squatted, rolling my eyes upward toward the treetops. God, I wanted to be back in England.

"I'm not saying we should take pleasure in killing her or hurting her," Elsa inhaled. Her arms twitched like she wanted to hold herself again, but she resisted. "We need to do what we can to... not die. That's all."

I suppose the worse alternative to dying a grisly death like Kaida was starving out in the woods alone. None of us wanted that — had pictured that for our summer vacation — and, I think, there were a few of us who enjoyed living enough to pick up a knife to survive. We were wary of the girl who'd started it all by trying to kill her sister, but there we were, entertaining the very same thing. I hated it. It was all a mess — and at the centre of that mess, *presto chango*, was my girlfriend.

"Guys," Byron finally said, "someone, um, got into Kaida's grave."

We'd all been avoiding looking at it. Like a dull full-stop, we finally stared at the disturbed shallow mound. It had been completely undone. Her body was gone, bones and all.

Esme

I bathed in a lake at the heart of the small lands, dipping my head beneath the crystalline surface, holding my breath for as long as I could before I arched up for air. Where once my skin had glistened with blood, it now moved with the liquid sheen of my soaked hair, dark red like old clay earth. I pressed my fingers over my round cheeks, revelling again in how smooth my skin felt. How perfect. My naked breast prickled up to meet the cool evening air. I didn't feel uncomfortable. With the water parting like silk at my every stroke, my hunger briefly sated, I felt as ancient and steadfast as the surrounding woodlands. I was a part of them, now, and they were a part of me. When Kaida's molten flesh was gone, I'd cracked her bones and sucked at the marrow, bit at the shards until the spaces between my teeth ached. It was a sweet ache. I paid my respects to her in the only way that I could, as her killer.

My little red dress lay crumpled at the edge of the water, thrown across a set of wooden slats that rather uselessly marked where the lake began, overgrown now with wild grass tufts from decades of natural solitude. The sun was bending to kiss the horizon, scattering fragments of diamond-like gold over the ripples that I'd caused. It was so peaceful — so much more so than the crowded city, or home in a bedroom with my knees squeezed up against my chest, trying to be small under the blankets so that, just for once, I would feel in control of myself and everything around me. I waded back towards those slats, the misshapen fabric, and shifted up to sit on the blades of grass where they bent into the lake's maw. I swept my hair over one shoulder and combed my fingers through it, separating out the glossy strands so that they spewed small waterfalls onto my thighs.

I knew the hunger would not be gone for long. Already I could feel its warning pangs waking through my belly, reaching up through my ribs to grasp at my breasts. I wondered if it was something that could ever be fully satisfied, or if this was my lot in life now, to hunt and to hunt and to hunt. There was something sad about that. I couldn't even cherish one death as a treasure. I had to make it a commodity just to survive. I tilted my head back and sniffed the air, to see if I could still scent the warmth of my friends on the wafting breeze. It wasn't as strong there by the lake, outside of the woods where they stumbled ungracefully like toddlers who'd just learned to push up off their hands. There was no urgency to the waning smell, though. I knew where to find them. That was my control now — not their secrets, but my pact with the woods. The woods were as angry and bitter at their disrespect as I was, though the woods wanted to be left in peace. If I was left in peace, I would starve and die.

I closed my eyes and pictured their faces. I curled Hana into my palm and tucked her away safely, out of sight of my rabid hunger. While I sheltered her, I peered at the rest, lifting my head over Kaida's sanctified remains to consider my options. They huddled together to keep warm in the evening, the edges of their shirts riding up their torsos from frayed desperation. One of them kept a little away from the rest, buzzing with nervous energy. I focused on him.

Back in my college dorm, sometime after Kaida's father started paying me for being his daughter's prettiest, most available friend, I came back to find that my door was ajar. I thought my roommate had forgotten to close it behind her, but I nudged it open to find a masculine back turned to me, hunched over my dresser, greedy fingers dabbling between flimsy underclothes. It wasn't the first time I'd come face to face with Byron Hughes, but I'd never gotten to know him before that. He was the sort that spoke up a lot in class, and who was good to have as a partner in a project, but I always thought he was a bit posh and off-putting. I suppose I'd gotten used to being leered at a certain way by boys, too, that I'd just brushed that off and taken it for granted. Maybe I should've worked on my radar a little more if his leering was going to progress to a complete invasion of privacy. I'd always thought about what I'd do in these kinds of situations. Maybe that's why I didn't react too loudly, or scream, or yell to the world at large what a creep he was. I just shut the door, letting its full weight swing it into the latch. He leapt up at the slam with a sickening, pink-cheeked shame that ran as deep as the length of his boner, which wasn't much.

"I can explain," he said, with half my panties hanging out of the dresser drawer. I let my schoolbag fall onto the floor with a similar, emphasised *thud*.

"It's fascinating what boys will ruin their lives for," I mused. It was the kind of thing you rehearsed saying in your head, over and over, trying to convince yourself that you weren't, well — a victim. His Adam's apple bobbed, and I could see more of the whites of his eyes than the rest of him.

I wondered, briefly, what he was capable of to maintain innocence.

"It's not what it looks like," he said, his white teeth gnashing. "I think I — I lost a pen in your bag when we met up for the assignment. D'you remember? You — you asked me to take out a paper —"

"Elsa did. I didn't. Why would your pen be in my dresser if it fell into *Elsa's* bag?"

His lip wobbled. That was it — the pathetic realisation that he'd fucked all his bright opportunities up because he was such a horny little shit. I felt it then, too — that twinge of power. He hung his head, his hands clenching and unclenching at his sides. I threw back my head and laughed. It fucked with him even more, me laughing. He had no idea what to do or say.

"You know," I said, "there's a few more assignments coming up that I could use some help with."

His eyes battled for space outside of his skull. "There aren't any more group projects left this semester. I checked." Why had he checked? To confirm if this was his last chance to drum up an excuse to break into my dorm room?

"No. But you get really good grades, Byron, outside of the group projects."

We stared at each other. For being such a bright pupil, it took an embarrassingly long while for him to understand what I was trying to say.

The pink on his cheeks deepened, but the way he shuffled said that he was relieved I was playing dirty, too. Because if I wasn't, the consequences would be a lot more dire for him.

He had that pink-cheeked, shuffling look to him then, huddling in the woods with all the rest of them, simmering with a shame that he'd kept buried for so long. I could smell it deeper than all of theirs combined, and I took a long, deep inhale. The hunger in my stomach curdled.

Satisfaction was so short-lived.

———————//———————

This hunt was different from the last. I had been angry with Kaida, with all of them, and wanted them to see my violence and fear me. I was almost gentle this time.

Byron wasn't sleeping. He tried, but because he thought it was safer to rest against a tree, the roots made his makeshift mattress uneven and too uncomfortable in his back. His stomach was empty, and he was full of resentment toward Cannon for discouraging a return to the cabin. He felt a lot of resentment for Cannon. Years at college, watching him intertwined with me, as friends, then as more, then as friends again. He pictured this suave American guy who had all his shit together, and yet had space to be maniacal under his flawlessness. He pictured this American twat sweeping in to charm the effortless English rose (me, though I was never this demure, opposite of a try-hard that Byron thought I was), and he had laid awake for nights on end with a jealousy that boiled to dangerous levels.

Then I needed his help (blackmailing him for help with my assignments), and he swept in. Then I fell in love with another girl, and oh — wasn't it all just a tragicomedy? But he didn't know what to feel toward Hana. Cannon was an easy target; Cannon reminded him that he fell short of the masculine ideal he thought he lacked. Hana was an error, a question mark that he couldn't compare himself to, and the thought of us together shamefully aroused him.

So, well, it was easier to keep riding the Cannon hate train.

With the amount he was mulling over it all that night, I think it would be easy to mistake his infatuation with me as an obsession with Cannon. Everything that he thought made him superior in comparison made him feel inferior. If Byron had had his way, he would be exactly like Cannon, and nothing like himself. The self-loathing in him wasn't sweet and dainty like the forced innocence in Kaida. It ran thick and greasy in his blood with the appeal of a fast-food joint. Cheap, but filling to the brim — and God, I was hungry again.

This hunt was different from the last — and dead easy. My hair still damp along my spine, I stood between the trees and watched him. He prided himself on noticing things around him that others did not. It was only a matter of time before he saw me. When he did, his eyes widened, his pulse quickened. The scent of him grew stronger and it was like he was already standing there in front of me, arms open wide to welcome the descent of my teeth. He scrambled, crawling towards me. He opened his mouth to wake the others, but I gently shook my head.

"I need you, Byron." *I need you, Byron*, his mind would place the emphasis. Finally, at last, the fragile rose picked him. *I've seen where I've fucked up all along. I swooned for all the wrong people.* His facial features relaxed, like he'd seen this coming for the whole trip. *Of course*, he would say to himself. *Of course things would resolve this way.*

He walked straight into me and I wrapped my hands around his throat, pulling him deeper into the woods. The adoration vanished out of his eyes. Finally, at long last, he saw me — *really* saw me. Not my tits or my lips or my hair, how nice I smelled, or anything like that. He saw beneath it all. Always wanting to get under my sheets, but ending straight under my skin.

I went under his, too.

alice

It wasn't difficult waking up. I'd never been a morning person really, but my stomach gnawed at itself, and my throat was so thick with dry, it felt like I'd had cotton wool stuffed down it. There was earth and leaf matted in my hair, usually so straight and shiny. I always got compliments on that: *Alice, your hair's so soft and shiny!* And Esme, with her loose waves, a sort of sandy beach texture, would curl her lip at me and look away. A lovely memory to wake up to.

I pushed myself up on one elbow, and I became distinctly aware that the human body can survive longer without food than it can without water. Whatever Cannon thought, we needed to go back to the cabin to at least get *water*. Facing down my sister was growing more and more appetising — or maybe that was just me starving. I rolled onto my knees, scrubbed the sleep out of my eyes, and peered toward the base of the tree where Byron had insisted on sleeping the night before.

He wasn't there.

A cold flash ran through me. I thought about Kaida and how her body disappeared from her shallow burial mound. I stumbled to my feet and glanced around at the others who were awake, but too exhausted to get up. "Byron's not here," I said, a little wildly. Cannon looked up at me. It took a moment for his eyes to register who I was. He pushed himself up, too, blearily. He was looking worse and worse for wear every morning.

"Maybe he went to, you know, relieve himself?" He ran a hand over one half of his face, digging the heel of his palm into his unruly stubble. I redirected myself toward Hana, feeling annoyed with him.

"Hana. Byron's gone." She was sitting up, her hands supporting the base of her spine, eyes wide and alert. She was on her feet quickly, too. She had a runner's body, slender and powerful. I think Esme used to tell me she did marathons or something.

"*Byron!*" she yelled, and Cannon groaned. Elsa was sitting up now, too, a quiet frown on her brow. I followed after Hana, my stomach revolting against every movement. "Byron, *where are you?*" Nothing answered her. That was the off-putting part of the woods — we never heard any birds. We never saw any signs of wildlife. Cannon used to say that was how you knew there was a tornado coming back home in America — when the birds left, and all that remained was silence.

"Do you think...?" I swallowed, unable to finish the sentence. Hana turned to me, her face pale and taut.

"I don't know. Wouldn't we have heard something? He'd put up a fight, right?"

"Unless she got him in his sleep. But then why wouldn't she go after the rest of us?" I gnawed at my bottom lip. That was what vexed me. If she was somehow in cahoots with the forest, we were surely dead meat from the moment we'd escaped into it. Why let us wander around, then, ambling for help? Did she know we were just that useless at navigating? Was she content to watch us struggle and then pick us off one by one? Hana looked a little sick with the thought. I wonder which hurt worse: knowing your sister was responsible for all this or knowing your girlfriend was.

"We have to keep looking," Hana decided, but at that moment Cannon caught up with us. He had a sort of shade of grey to his once healthy skin. A lack of sleep and nutrition was making him look as strung out as Esme would have us believe he was normally.

"Hey, no, we have to stick to the plan. If we go wandering around willy-nilly, we'll lose ourselves again." Not that we'd made particular progress, winding back exactly to where Kaida was buried. I suppose he had a point, though. At least we made more progress the day before than we had when we first started. I looked uncertainly at Hana and saw a more open irritation pass through her face.

"I'm not sure if you noticed, but one of your friends is missing. Maybe we should make sure he isn't, I don't know, *dead*?"

Cannon breathed an incredulous laugh at the word 'friends', and I remembered how Esme used to gloat that Byron had "such a huge thing" for her. When I asked why he seemed so jealous of Cannon, she'd tossed her head and said, "Isn't it obvious, Alice? The guy wants to fuck me."

He studied the trees for a moment. "Be honest, Hana. After seeing what she... what she was, how she was like in the cabin... you really want to go out there and risk yourself for a guy you barely know?"

Elsa and Finn came up behind him, the former with her arms shielded about herself again, and the latter openly concerned. He looked between Cannon and us, silently beseeching for an explanation.

"Yeah, actually," Hana snapped. "Seeing my girlfriend go a little crazy doesn't stop me from caring about other people's lives, funnily enough."

"A *little* crazy? Be serious, Hana. You didn't run for your life out the front door and leave us all behind just because she went *a little crazy*."

"Are you for real? Are you holding against me the fact that I went looking for *help*?"

"Yeah, you really succeeded. Just ran a big ol' circle —"

"*Cannon*," Elsa snapped. "Back off."

We fell silent. What were we even without Esme to anchor us? They all barely concealed the fact that they despised each other. I felt sorry for them, and then I felt sorry for me — but most of all I felt sorry for Hana. If she hadn't bumped into Esme at that bookstore, she wouldn't be here. She'd be happy, spending her summer holiday somewhere else, with nicer people. I paused and thought about it some more. Was I being too generous? All the guilt that I'd been harbouring wasn't just because I'd picked up a knife and tried to kill my sister, it was because I felt that I'd *succeeded*. I *had* killed her, and that had led to this awful reincarnation of her as something far worse than she'd ever been in life. Why should I pity myself if I was responsible?

Was that why she was picking us off one by one? Was she trying to send me a message? That was something Esme would do to really get under my skin. The kind of big-sister-poking-fun-at-her-little-sister-just-a-bit-too-hard — *no Alice, she didn't mean it like that. She's your sister. She cares about you.* My dad's troubled face, because he didn't believe his own words. I swallowed, the cotton wool-y feeling only doubling as I did.

"I'll go. If you guys don't want to, I can go."

Now they all looked at me, incredulous. Even Cannon, who just yesterday had been touting how it was all my fault.

"Don't be stupid, Alice." Hana shook her head. "Losing you too isn't going to help us find Byron."

"Think about it, though. I'm the one who — who kicked this whole thing off, right? With the knife?" I swallowed again, and again my throat just thickened all the more. "Who do you think she'd choose to go after, then? Me, or the lot of you?"

A shadow of contemplation fell over Cannon's face. Maybe that was cheeky of me, a bit, playing into what I knew he wanted to hear. I told myself it was for the good of all of them. That it was noble. Was it noble if I stood there thinking how noble it was? Hana only doubled down, though, her jaw squaring.

"We're not *sacrificing* you. Just like we're not sacrificing Byron. Let's just — knock it off and go find him. Right, guys?" She looked to Elsa and Finn for support. What she received back were two guilty stares. Hana bristled. "Oh, Christ. Not you two as well? Honestly. Do any of you actually *give a shit* about each other? Or are you all as fake as Esme said you were?"

"You already know she's no paragon saint," Elsa said quietly. Hana's face flushed.

"I know — I know that the girl I started dating wouldn't just leave any of her friends to die. I know I wouldn't do that. Hell, *I* wouldn't do that for a stranger."

"The girl you started dating started murdering us." Cannon sucked in his cheeks. "Maybe you don't know as much as you think, Hana Baily."

They were going to descend into arguing and bickering again. There wasn't any time for that. I didn't want this to go on any longer than it had to. I breathed in, filling my chest. I dragged my feet backwards, slowly. I don't know why I thought I could just sneak away. Hana's head whipped towards me.

"Alice, don't."

"I'm sorry," I gushed out quickly, releasing all the air I'd built up inside of me. Then, like I was a little kid again about to get in trouble when Esme saw I'd made a hole in one of her favourite shirts, I turned and ran.

It felt silly at first, my feet tangling in the uneven ground, toes knotting over roots. I remembered too late, again, that Hana was good at running. She came after me in a quick flurry, practically soundless compared to my clumsy stumbling. She grabbed my arm, and I yanked it back as petulant as I felt.

"You can't be serious," she said. When I looked at her over my shoulder, I realised she had come after me alone. There was a pang of loneliness at that. I hadn't taken to my sister's friends, but I'd hoped they still cared for me in a weird way. My nobility felt stupid all of a sudden, but I reminded myself that everything that had felt stupid and unreal in the past couple of days had turned out to become our grounded reality.

"Dead serious." Maybe I'd just be plain *dead*, soon enough. "Think about it — whenever we wander the woods without marking where we've been, where do we always end up?"

Hana's brow knotted. "The cabin."

"If Byron wandered off — and I'm not saying he isn't smart, but it's not promising to wander off into the woods like that, given everything that's happened. He probably wasn't as careful as we've been. So... he'll probably end up back at the cabin." I could feel a feverish flush in my cheeks as I explained, as though I had to prove myself to Hana before I continued on my quest. Stupid, really. She watched me closely, like I was about to erupt onto something concerning — something straitjacket-worthy. "Well... what I'm trying to say is, chances are I'll end up back at the cabin too. I might find Byron. I might be able to get us some food and — I might be able to talk sense into her. She's my sister. I started this."

"Not to sound like Cannon, but have you *seen* what she's capable of, Alice?"

I had. I'd watched her tear out Kaida's throat. You'd never think the worst person you know would be capable of that. I swallowed slowly, once again trying to will that dried cotton sensation away.

"That's why I have to stop it all." I looked over her shoulder, willing her to go back to the others, but I couldn't see them. I frowned. "Where'd they go?"

She looked, too, with a sort of infuriated huff through her nose, probably thinking I was about to run off again. Then she became very still.

"Well," she said. "Fuck."

Hana

One memorable thing about Byron — whenever we got onto the subject of horror films (he was a film buff, I guess) he'd always tout that the number one rule was to stick together. He took great pleasure in deriding those foolhardy protagonists who got distracted and wandered off, then when they looked back over their shoulder — *oh*, here comes a rockslide to separate them from the rest of the party! "It makes it easier for the monster to pick them off," Byron would say, rolling his eyes exaggeratedly. "C'mon, one or two teenagers aren't going to put up much of a fight compared to... well, strength in numbers and all that."

So, anyway, sincerely fuck Byron from the bottom of my heart for wandering off. And fuck me, too. And fuck Alice to a lesser extent. She was trying to be a hero, yes, but it was somehow less annoying than when Cannon did it. She had this little spark in her eye and I think when she said she was going to have a talk with her sister, she meant she was going to try and kill her again.

Maybe it was less that it wasn't as annoying and more that I was a little afraid of this seventeen-year-old with a plan.

The woods stretched out on either side of us, tall thin trees with fallen brethren and lashing roots spaced between them, clusters of leaves but no sign of our friends. I was dumbfounded. Had they turned and ran from *us* as well, or had I chased Alice further than I thought? Why hadn't they come after us both? It was like I was the only person who had ever listened to Byron's horror film warnings. I twisted about futilely on my feet, looking this way and that, before my slight companion finally sucked in one cheek and chided, "We're lost already, Hana. That's the point. You shouldn't have run after me."

"You shouldn't have *run* full-stop! This isn't a game, Alice. This isn't just you and Esme having a little domestic. She's *killing* people."

"But she won't hurt *you*," Alice replied, her foot tapping like she was being generously patient with me by explaining all this. "My plan won't work if you're with me. She'll go after the others. I know she will."

"I think you're *vastly* overestimating how valuable my life is to her."

"I'm *not*. Dracula by Bram Stoker."

I paused, staring at her like she'd gone mad, which she might well have. "What?"

"Dracula *by Bram Stoker*. That's the book you were holding when she first saw you. Ask me how I know."

"So, she told you how she met me. I don't understand how that's relevant."

Alice sighed, long-suffering. "She bragged to me about *everything*. All the dirt she had on her friends. All the ways she was using them to her benefit. She hated me, but she wanted me to know how much better she had it, right?" She paused. "When she talked about you, all she talked about were the good things. Dracula, how you ate lunch on the steps leading up to your dorms, how you're great at running, how you're not like anyone else she's met. You understand how significant that is, right, for someone who keeps track of every less than perfect thing people do around her?"

I wanted to believe it, but I thought of what Elsa had said again — I simply hadn't known her long enough for her to sink her claws into me. Everyone had secrets; something they were a little ashamed of, no matter how big or slight. I didn't need to have had a dark, awful secret for Esme to have found something to manipulate me with. To say that I had to have one was to imply that the rest of them were at fault for ever having lived, for ever having been taken advantage of, or made a mistake, or... I couldn't, in good conscience, allow myself to think that I was the only exception. It was flawed, it felt sticky, and I didn't want to depend on being in Esme's good graces anymore, no matter how *good* it had made me feel at any other time. "It doesn't matter," I told her. "She killed Kaida in front of me, remember? I was there. You were there, too, and she didn't gun straight for *you*."

The determination in Alice's face faltered. I almost felt bad. A part of me also felt it was useless, because despite everything, we had become separated. Even if she ran back her plan now, there was no guarantee we'd be able to find everyone again. I looked at the trees, perplexed that these were unmarked. A sinking part of me wondered if Esme had torn the strips of shirt away from the bark, just to make us suffer all the more — or maybe the trees themselves had shed those man-made markers in an act of pure contempt. It didn't beggar belief, the thought that the woods loathed us.

"You agree we need food though, right?" Alice stared at me with her round eyes, gnawing on one half of her own lip. "Water, too. I'm parched."

That one, I couldn't deny. My stomach was running on pure adrenaline and my voice felt like it was going to crack with every vowel. Not to mention the pounding dehydration headache, which wasn't doing me any favours in the realm of *thinking*. Of course, that meant going back to the cabin. I thought of the blood in the kitchen, then the blood in the dining room. My empty stomach did flip-flops. "You have to promise me you won't run off again. Promise you won't try to get yourself killed." Or what? I'd be grumpy the whole way to the cabin? Thankfully, Alice didn't see through the bluff like I did — or maybe she did, and she was good at concealing it. She bobbed her red head up and down, and I suddenly saw the resemblance there between her and her sister. The whisper of the auburn-haired mother they'd shared, who'd instilled that complex knife of womanhood in the two of them.

"Do you think we'll be able to find the others again?" she asked quietly. I licked my cracked lips.

"I'm sure it won't be too hard. Just keep an ear out for Cannon barking military drills."

Hey. I got a smile out of her.

Alice

It didn't take long for us to find the cabin again. It was as I thought — you set out in any direction and just let your feet carry you. The woods lead you back to it. Where Hana thought it was out of contempt, I wondered if the trees wanted to protect us as well. *You don't belong here*, they seemed to say. *You belong there.* And there was relief in me when I saw those domesticated four walls and the porch with its yellow-tinged light, the circle of Elsa's discarded cigarette butts not so far away. The comfortable human recognition of *shelter* gave temporary reprieve to the doubling ache of hunger and the choking of thirst.

We weren't graceful. We rushed inside and tried not to look at the signs of violence that had happened there. We stopped in the bathroom and took turns drinking from the tap. The more I drank, the more I felt the coldness fill up the hollow of my stomach. Sooner or later, I would have to enter the kitchen again — the room that had started it all. I hovered just shy of the shower and Hana looked at me, moisture dripping from her lips.

"What's wrong?" she asked, alert, like she thought maybe I'd heard Esme walking down the hallway toward us. I don't know why, but it felt to us both, then, that the cabin was deserted — a safe haven rather than a prison. That meant she was out in the woods with our friends, but we didn't want to think on that.

"I'm hungry," I said lamely. For a moment, I was back at home and looking up at my dad, still in his work clothes, poised in the kitchen and cracking open something cold from the refrigerator. He looked alarmed that he had woken me; worried, with the crease of a frown cutting through his brow. At my childish answer, he would relax. *Want a peanut butter and jelly?* he'd ask conversationally, moving about the countertops with the ease of familiarity. I'd draw a stool up and nod, and in watching him go through the practised motions, I'd feel safe again for one night. I blinked, and it was Hana in front of me again. She had straightened and was dragging the back of her wrist across her mouth.

"Come on," she said, a little more hushed. I was sure — so sure — that Esme wasn't in the cabin, but I appreciated her guard. We crept together from the bathroom, moving through the dining — and that's when we recoiled, seeing the first signs of blood streaked across the walls. Kaida's, but maybe it had trailed from Cannon's dragging hand. Finn's shoulder bumping against the walls after her torn throat had rested briefly on his sleeve. It occurred to me then how fucked up it must have been for them — must *still* be for them — carrying someone between them who had died only hours later. Hana reached back and grabbed me by the wrist (maybe she'd meant to grab my hand, I don't know) and we moved into the kitchen with our chins pushed out and our hearts leaping in our chests.

The kitchen looked so tame. It had no right to look so tame. I'd tried to kill my sister in that very room. She'd pretty much killed Kaida there. It was empty, though, and if I wasn't so ravenous, maybe it would have ruined my appetite. We walked clumsily to the fridge and dug for something quick and easy to eat. Though, maybe we wouldn't have minded biting into the frozen meats we'd bought to cook up for a barbeque. *Barbeque.* We'd really thought we were going to have a normal, fun summer.

"Here," Hana said. She'd uncovered a pack of salty caramel cheese that we'd found in Gothenburg and been curious to try. *From the mountains of Norway*, it boasted. It wasn't even a Swedish delicacy. We ripped open the package and stuffed the slices into our mouth, not taking a moment to appreciate the flavour. It didn't feel enough, but it was perfect at the same time. Maybe if we'd gotten our hands on something heavier, we'd just end up heaving and sick. As we ate, we avoided looking around us. Our eyes were blank and dissociated, our forms crouched and greedy. My sister would have been proud of us, I'm sure, if she'd seen.

When the packet was empty, we rocked back on our heels and sat crosslegged on the bare floorboards, studying the kitchen in a vague stupor. This was our reality, from stumbling about the woods to revisiting our friend's murder scene. I wondered which blood streak was Kaida's and which was my sister's. I suppose Esme's would have browned by then. I started picking at the wood on the floorboards, seeing if I could scrape up anything under my fingernail.

"Byron's not here." I'd forgotten we were looking for him like an idiot, I was so hungry, but that was the first thing Hana said as she looked contemplatively around. I thought she'd make a good nurse; she was so at ease amidst the carnage.

"Neither's Esme." We looked at each other. "Do you think she...?"

"We can't know. Byron used to say that. Can't know someone's dead unless you see the body."

"Isn't that for like, movies and stuff?"

One corner of Hana's mouth twisted up in half-feigned amusement. "This is *kind of* a film." If it was a film, I wished it was flashier, with good music. I wished we would cut away from the gristle and gore smoothly — transition into a hopeful scene where we stumble onto another cabin and oh, us the final girls, we arrange a rescue and get everything sorted. There would be the climactic showdown, but we would come out of it with blood-stained bravado. My sister would smile softly and whisper an apology as she became herself again. *You'll always be my baby sister*, she'd say, and gently touch my cheek. This wasn't a film, though, and Esme would sooner call me a cunt. No matter how many times I blinked, none of the blood faded to black.

"Maybe we should get what food we can and try to find the others again," I said after a while. I think maybe my plan was bullshit. I think maybe Esme was too far gone to pick and choose who she was going to go after next. I caught Hana looking wistfully toward the doorway of the kitchen, past the dining room. Maybe she was imagining the bed she'd shared with Esme just nights ago. Maybe she was picturing the vacation we could have had.

"Yeah," she said finally. "Let's get out of here."

ESMIE

Esme

At least they were just as quick to turn on each other as they were to turn on me. They hadn't mourned me, and they hadn't mourned Byron. God, they'd *barely* mourned Kaida. It made the hunt feel justified to me in my nightmare haze. How could they, in good conscience, call themselves friends? I wasn't an orbit which they couldn't pull away from. If they didn't like each other, or me, they could have simply *fucked off* at any time. But no. They were poor, sweet victims, and I the monster. *I* was the one who got assaulted in the kitchen! *I* was the one who felt my throat get cut!

I watched them let Hana peel away. They let the woods swallow her up and they just stood there like cunts and did nothing. I was furious with them. They could hate each other and themselves all they liked, but Hana — sweet Hana — hadn't done anything wrong. God, they'd barely given themselves a chance to know her. They didn't run after her. They didn't go to see if she was all right. They just stood there, and, after a while, Cannon said in his stupid, exaggerated drawl, "Well. That's that." *That's that.* What a piece of shit. What a full-of-himself piece of shit.

Cannon Moody was the very thing you pictured when someone said the words *frat boy*. An arm-pumping pustule of limbs with a paper cup full of vodka somewhere in that mess, smiley faces on his tongue, and glazed, dead-fish eyes before he leaned in to kiss you. I didn't feel anything when Cannon and I started dating. It felt more like I was fulfilling a prophecy.

Hot, magnetic college girl meets carefree, Los Angeles-chic party boy. What happens? Sex, probably. Power couple, whatever. But I felt nothing for him. And the more I fed him the pills that I had — that I could wrap my pinky finger around — the more I saw him for what he was — not particularly impressive.

So, we broke up. That's fine — we worked better as friends. We could actually have in-jokes and hang out without pressure, and I didn't have to see his fisheyes when he leaned into me anymore. He still showed up at my dorm in the little hours, asking for pills, for weed, for a little drink from my stash. Those were tolerable annoyances in the pretty uneventful canvas that was our friendship. Even if I wasn't dating him, I got a little bit of the prestige that came with rubbing shoulders with *the cute American*. All my girlfriends made goo-goo eyes at him, muttered something about girl code, and I'd go, *What? Go fuck him already.* And they did. And, you know, they never stuck around.

I wasn't the problem is what I'm trying to say.

It pissed me off that he had the gall to stand there, wash his hands of my girlfriend, and say *that's that*. I knew he got a little jealous about us, but I didn't realise he was so fucking petty. God, I wanted to strangle him.

God, I *could* strangle him.

"That's that?" Elsa spat out — practically *gurgled* it. Her face was drawn and white. I'd seen that look from her before. It came when she was at the end of her rope. And, oh, she was about to let loose on the worst boyfriend of the year. "What the — what the *fuck* is even happening? We just lost half our friends!"

"We can't let them go off alone," Finn said. Nice, kind Finn, who usually kissed Cannon's ass for as long as he could, to make up for the fact that he couldn't *literally* do it. At least he'd never been jealous of me. I respected that about him. Cannon seemed offended that they were questioning his word of law — because he thought that's what he was then, some Texas preacher in a mobile church amidst all that damp Swedish woods and pagan roots. Maybe his condescension came from thinking he led some crusade. Maybe he'd like to put Hana and I up as two witches; two blinking lights of his humiliation.

"They just did," he said, like he was explaining to two children the birds and the bees. "And frankly, that's their choice. If they wanna... wanna go after the incel with no survival instinct, they can be my guest."

"Incel?" Finn echoed. He was *shocked*, poor thing, that Cannon thought so low of maybe anyone. I could picture the halo being knocked off from up above the preacher's head, all broken neon signage, flickering amongst the wires. Elsa powered through like none of that mattered. She was good at sniffing out what mattered and what didn't.

"If you wanted to stay alive, chasing everyone away until you're the only one left isn't the *smart* way to do it."

"Oh, yeah?" Cannon swung close to her, sunken eyes and ripped up shirt, wiry like he still had all those pills jumping through his veins. He always came to class so exhausted and dehydrated, he probably didn't know the difference. "Maybe that's all right. Seems I'm the only one with *sense* enough to know that going back to that cabin is just *asking* to be killed. Going after some guy who'd follow Esme's tits to the end of the earth? Guess what? We're gonna find Esme's tits. Only that ain't Esme no more. That's some — that's some —"

"I don't fucking care what she is! *You're* going crazy!"

"Okay, why didn't you go with Hana, then? Huh? You seemed perfectly fine letting the two of them go when you could stand behind me and let *me* take all the blame. Just like you're perfectly fine blaming how fucked up you are on Esme, when the truth is —"

"*What?*" Elsa Lagerlöf squared up to the man a quarter of her height taller than her, jutting her chin out like it was a gun. "Go on, party boy. Tell me what the goddamn truth is."

"Stop," Finn said, somewhere between the two of them. He took turns looking between them and the trees, desperate. "Stop, this isn't getting us anywhere."

"When the truth is she was just a scapegoat," Cannon tore through gritted teeth. "The only person you've to blame for being all messed up in the head, all used up, Lagerlöf, is yourself."

Everything was still. The birds don't sing here, and the trees just watched. I watched too. I watched the muscles in Elsa's jaw work and work. I watched her eyes grow bright with anger and frustration and, the best of all, hatred. I thought, well, *finally* — finally she could understand how I'd felt. Why I was the way I was, and, for a moment, I was sad that she hadn't arrived there sooner. Maybe we could have bonded, and maybe something genuine could have come of our friendship. She slowly wet her lips and shook her head. If I was her, I wouldn't have let him get away with that, of course. I'd scratch his eyes out. Punch him in the gut. Grab him by the throat and…

They looked up at me, suddenly. I'd gotten too aroused by the thought, and the branch cracked beneath me. Their eyes were wide, reflecting back the faint light that was peering through the clouds. Gone was the hatred, the anger, the argument. Everything was still, and I didn't like the stillness because it felt too real. I didn't want any of it to be real.

The branch gave way, and I went with it, my feet crashing onto Cannon's shoulders, my hands latching around his jaw. His blood sprayed on poor Elsa as I tore his throat clean off, sinews and all. It painted her like she was Carrie; got in her hair, in her pretty lashes. When she screamed, it even landed on her tongue. She recoiled from me, wet strands of gore clinging to her cheeks, her hands rising up to cover her face. Her heel dragged over uneven ground, catching on a root. She fell backwards into Finn. Cannon's head was in my palms, his pale eyes staring sightlessly up into the trees. My fingers cloyed around his sharp cheeks, familiar to my touch. I felt a pang then — just a pang — of an affection that had never fully taken root. It was the potential, I think. There's nothing sadder than missed potential. My stomach churned and roiled, and the sadness deepened. Was it ever going to stop?

"Elsa," Finn was saying. I looked at him, and he looked back with unmasked horror, nausea, grief. He'd never looked at me like that before. My gentle friend, who'd only ever befriended me to get closer to Cannon — but a friend anyway. He'd never ever looked at me like that. "Elsa, run. *Run!*"

Stop, I wanted to say. *Stop please, I don't know how to stop it — the hunger, the everything — don't look at me like that. Don't look at me like that.* Cannon's head dropped from my palms. It rolled towards them, and they parted, screaming, leaping away from each other. Without thinking, they scrambled toward different directions. *Don't*, I wanted to say again. *Don't trust the woods.* What came out was something haggard, something deeper than my chest. I reached out, and

I didn't recognise my hand. My perfect, glistening red hand.

What was I? No, this was a dream. This was a dream. This was all a bad *fucking* dream.

Uncle Rowan said so. Uncle Rowan always fucking said so.

And I was so *fucking* hungry.

I grabbed my travel bag from the bedroom I'd been sharing with Esme not so long ago. The four-poster looked stupid and harmless now that it was empty. It was one of those quaint ones with the soft drapes and intricate wood headboard — something that made you feel like cottagecore royalty when you slept inside of it. I stared at it and remembered my girlfriend sitting on my chest. It was hard to swallow. I touched the covers. It had long rows of faded pink roses printed down its grain. If I closed my eyes, I could imagine a different vacation, with different people — my mum, for instance, would look down at those covers. She wouldn't particularly like them, but she'd say, *Now that's good quality*. She'd also call them *quaint*. She'd smile and she'd feel silly. It's a nice place that would make my hard-working mother feel silly.

"Hey."

My eyes opened. Alice was hovering in the doorway, holding up her own bag. She twisted her mouth from side to side. I guess she didn't want to be alone for too long. I couldn't really blame her.

"Sorry," I said. "Drifted off." I retrieved my hand from the faded rose print and drew my bag over one shoulder. There were toiletries rattling around in there, but otherwise there was plenty of space to fill it up with perishables. My main concern was finding our group again. The woods weren't exactly taking it easy on us. Kind of pathetic, right, how our aim had gone from finding help to just being able to find one another?

"It's okay." Alice stared round-eyed at the four-poster, like she'd never seen one before in her life. "You know, Esme kicked up a fuss about getting this room. But it's nice."

"Yeah. I get it, though. The boys are loud."

"I've never seen her *not* get her way before." Alice huffed a little. "Elsa's kind of a badass."

Elsa *was* kind of a badass. I felt a sudden surge of respect towards her. Maybe after all of this was over, we needn't all have to hate each other. Maybe I could salvage *some* friendships from this trainwreck. I'd never gotten to know Elsa properly, nor Alice, nor Finn... maybe there was something there. Something that orbited free of Esme.

Something rattled in the kitchen and we both froze. Up until then, we'd operated under the impression that we were alone in the cabin. Suddenly, I felt stupid and overly confident. Then I felt stupid for being so scared of my girlfriend. Then I remembered that she wasn't really my girlfriend — not anymore. She probably wasn't even really human. I gestured to Alice to get behind me. She squared her jaw and walked beside me instead.

The kitchen was as we left it, dried blood streaks and all. We stood foolishly in the archway that led from the dining area, our bags swinging harmlessly at our sides. We exchanged looks. There was the unspoken, *Maybe it was nothing*, but we didn't want to voice it in case it jinxed us. I tossed my head toward the refrigerator.

"Let's —"

"*Yeah.*"

We squatted in front of the humming appliance, cold air blasting on our faces as we fit as much plastic packaging in our hands as we could in one pass. Even the raw, frozen meats that would have to be grilled to be edible. Bear Grylls had drank his own piss once; we couldn't afford to be choosy. Maybe the clatter of the shelves inside disguised any further noise. Maybe we willed ourselves not to hear anything until our bags were full. The moment I slammed the door shut, I heard the slide of *something* over the floorboards. I grabbed Alice's hand and turned around.

A giant snake was wending its way over the abandoned countertops, scooting over shards of plate, rolling glasses on their sides. It moved like liquid and its dark scales had the greasy sheen of an oil slick pooling on the ground. My heart, and then bile, leapt up into my throat. It was coming straight for us, guiding itself with the apex of its nose, silently hunting.

"Oh, gawd," Alice squeaked. I pushed at her, but the snake reared up suddenly, coming above us. It opened its mouth, showing fleshy pink cheek meat and sharp, fine-pointed teeth. A horrible, distorted baby's cry tore out of that slick maw, gushing over my face with the sweet milk scent of new skin and baby powder that I'd encountered once, maybe twice, in my life. Alice gagged at my shoulder.

"Out," I said. "Outout*out*." My pushes turned to shoves, and then we were stumbling over each other, tracing clumsy circles around a massive snake that was screaming and wailing like a newborn. Sweat had sprung up in little pools in the crevices of my palms, but the surface of my skin was freezing. I wanted to vomit. I was *going* to vomit. We careened out of the kitchen into the little bathroom hallway, then out through the door and past Elsa's cigarette butt circle. Alice was swearing — or was that me? We were holding onto each other's forearms at that point, and we pivoted simultaneously to stare wide-eyed back at the cabin, waiting to see if the creature had followed us. I could still hear it wailing, faintly — like it really was a baby, cursed to crawling about the cabin, searching for someone, anyone, to feed it.

"What the fuck?" Alice whisper-screamed. She was shaking like a leaf. "What the *fuck*?" Watching Esme completely lose her mask of civility was one thing — that snake was *actually* inhuman. It was *actually* monstrous. Reality had been bent over the countertop and snapped in two. I felt queasy; my head was swimming. It was like we were back in the dining area drinking that weird peachy cocktail Cannon had mixed up. I inhaled sharply.

"I'm going to puke."

"What the *fuck*."

I squatted and emptied the torn-up shreds of cheese onto the stubby little grass that was shy of the forest. Most of it was bile, of course, since I hadn't eaten in days. It stung my throat and had me gagging for a few seconds more.

"Hana, we can't — let's go, okay? Let's just go."

I hurried to wipe the stinging acid from my lips. I was already moving toward the treeline on my knees. Alice helped me up the rest of the way and we stumbled through the rough bark shield. Twigs and leaf cracked underfoot. I was beginning to hate that noise.

"What was that?" she asked me, like I had confidential information. "What the fuck *was* that?"

"I don't know." I was doggedly setting my sight on the trees in front of us, looking for shirt strips. If we didn't find shirt strips, we were going to follow the ones that didn't, I decided. If we couldn't find our friends, we would find help. This time, I wouldn't fail.

"Hana — *Hana!*"

Alice dragged me to a stop, planting her heels on the earth while pulling at my wrist. I turned back around to her with wide, unfocused eyes. I hadn't realised I was hyperventilating. She wasn't doing much better.

"Listen. Is it following us?" Her breaths gushed out one hot puff after the other. I strained my ears to listen. The wailing seemed the same distance as it had been before, but there was something else layered on top of it. Sobbing? That seemed even closer. I swallowed.

"Elsa? Elsa, is that you?"

It was unmistakeable — the sobs were getting closer. I could hear physical, tangible footsteps crushing twig and leaf underfoot. The more I looked about, though, the more I could only see close-knit trees, standing steadfastly tall all the way out. Which was bullshit, by the way, since we'd only just run into the woods. We were being fucked with again. I could feel it deep in my bones.

"That's not Elsa," Alice whispered. She started pulling me in the opposite direction. But when we pivoted, the sobbing sounded like it moved with us. "Oh, that's not fair."

"No," I heard myself say. "No, we have to keep moving. This is what it wants, for us to stand still. We have to keep moving."

"Which way? Hana, which —"

A sob fell and stopped just behind us. It was so close, I could hear the hiccupping breath as it subsided. The hairs stood up on the back of my neck.

"Babes?" a familiar voice said, cracking and quavering. "Babes, it's me."

——— // ———   𝒜   ——— // ———

Esme

Elsa wasn't as fast or elegant a runner as Hana. She was model skinny, and maybe she'd have been picked up by an agency if she wasn't short, too. She was all angles and bones jutting out, and skin discoloured to a bruise-like hue where it was too thin against her joints. Now she was streaked with dirt and leaf and blood down her face and in her hair and all over her cardigan. She ran and she ran and didn't look back, and it took too long for her to realise that she was all alone.

She crashed into a tree — I felt it shudder through me. I was the woods and the woods were me. We watched her, bemused. My hunger was briefly sated on Cannon. She had nothing to fear for now. She hugged the bark, and she sobbed and swore, and it was the most emotion I had ever seen out of her. It was mesmerising.

Elsa was the kind of girl all the college boys called *frigid*. They'd congregated around her because she was pretty, and then they moved on to making fun of her for being too uptight. It was all the recipe an apex predator needed to sniff out an easy kill. So, she got a boyfriend and swam in and out of my periphery in a soft, blushing ball. When her path crossed Cannon's and mine, we shared our pills with her. We hooked her onto weed. She didn't get addicted like my ex-boyfriend, but it was enough that she let loose in a way I don't think she ever had before.

The relationship didn't last long. Silly college flings generally don't. The thing that stuck out though, was that Elsa's boyfriend had gotten into the habit of recording her when she was blackout drunk. Things she didn't consent to. They spread around the jeering college boys like wildfire, and her mental health went to shit. She became ten times worse than the 'frigid bitch' she had arrived as. I smelled it as soon as it happened, and I hunted down the source of her transformation.

I got her ex to get the videos offline, but I kept them. I never looked at them; I never wanted to. For all Elsa knew though, I was party to the whole thing. She thought I knew all the *secret websites* they had been uploaded to, when it had only been one. Generally, her ex shared the videos through private group chats. I got the back-ups sent to me. Maybe I was going to show them to her, say *look what I did*, but I just ended up keeping them. And then I brought it up once or twice, and… well, she hated me for it. She didn't know what I'd done, though. What I'd *really* done. And I did it for her.

Despite all that, this was the most fragile I had ever seen her. I suppose it wasn't every day that she got bathed in someone else's blood. Maybe that had never happened to her at all, come to think of it. She hugged the tree like it was a person ready to comfort her and she sobbed and choked on her own spit and bile. I almost felt sorry for her. There was a part of me that did, genuinely, but it was so distant from me, like a fairytale. Once upon a time in a faraway land, Elsa and I were friends. Once upon a time in a faraway land, I had fought for her right to feel comfortable in her own body again, but then ended up using it against her. The romantic in me suggested that maybe I just didn't want to lose her. What better way to keep someone you like close than to hold something embarrassing over their head? Friendships come and go, but trauma is forever.

At least, that's what I told myself at the time. And at that point, it was too late to retract.

She was whispering something to the tree. A prayer? It felt like a prayer — or a plea for forgiveness. Her tongue moved lusciously over her teeth, and I felt the branches around me soften. Here was a bastardised version of the language they once heard, and it rippled through them like a child's drawing would drift listlessly upon a breeze. She left smudges of blood on the bark from her fingertips. As she stumbled onward, I felt we had less animosity toward her — finally, *finally*, some respect. She sang under her breath as she moved, a sort of feverish, frantic whisper. Her eyes were wide and glassy; her lips squirmed quickly over shining teeth. *When mother troll has put her eleven small trolls to bed and bound them up in her tail, then she sings to the eleven small trolls the most beautiful words she knows.* "Ho, aj aj aj buff," she hissed to herself. "Ho, aj aj aj aj…" One foot in front of the other, on and on. Defiant and stubborn, the Elsa Lagerlöf I know. She didn't need markers on the trees, she decided. She simply wouldn't get lost. She simply wouldn't allow it.

///

Finn broke out of the trees, and instead of the cabin in front of him, he saw a meadow open up under his feet. At the far end was another redwalled hut with figures moving in and out of its precipice. His joy bubbled up through his throat, the trees disinterested in him now as he stumbled toward freedom. Finn Armstrong had never done me wrong — had only turned a blind eye to the faults of the boy he loved. He was the one who took Cannon Moody under his wing and *integrated him into English society*, or so they'd joke. What he meant was the party scene, the drugs, and then me. What Finn took for fun, Cannon learned to rely upon. Cannon was so good at covering that up, though. Finn never suspected. Maybe he should have — but he didn't. And even when I'd whipped up his favourite American boy and made him fall in love with *me*, he never held a hateful bone in his body. He buried the bitterness under a feeling of resignation familiar to those who are used to hiding aspects of themselves to survive. Still, I'd gotten him to do me favours simply by showing a little kindness to Cannon in turn. I suppose we both enabled him in the end.

Finn kept going, lifting up his lanky brown arms to wave and catch the attention of the pale, dumpling-like couple who had turned to squint towards him. Even in the summer, they wore long-sleeved shirts and sweeping bottoms, anything to hide their flesh from any potential burn. The man lifted a hand to his brow, the brim of his cap already jutting out and shading his eyes. Finn bravely called out,

"Please help! Please help! Something's happened to my friends!"

And of course they understood, because the rest of Europe had exasperatedly bowed its head to the little island of Britain, its corrupt English heart, and said, *All right, we'll speak your language.* The man turned and said something to his wife and Finn was afraid that meant they hadn't caught what he'd said.

"Please! I need — please —"

"Wait," the trees heard the man call. "Wait there."

"No," Finn said, desperate to get as far from us as possible. "Please." They met halfway through the grass, and it took everything in my old friend not to grab the man by his arms and just sink, sink, sink, until it was all just a distant memory. "There's something hunting my friends… we've been lost in the woods…"

Get the boys from the other cabin, the man said to his wife in the child-language. She wavered but then turned and hobbled off. "I hear you," he said to Finn, his voice thick in his throat. "I hear you. What is it? What is in the woods?"

Finn had no answer to that. How would he describe me now? How would he describe us? We are no longer the girl that he knew, and yet we are still the same. *I* am still the same. Fragments of me float between the leaves, a scream frozen in time, a throat gushing blood, a womb gushing blood. He choked on his words and the man stood as stiff as cardboard, unsure what to do with the English boy in front of him. He kept looking back over his shoulder, then back to Finn, then back over his shoulder. In the distance, the shape of a group surfaced — a collection of limber men, all pale-skinned and swaggering with familiarity.

For the first time in days, Finn let his breath out.

Hana

The voice belonged to my girlfriend. It had the soft Brummie accent, the condescending lilt — everything that hallmarked itself as Esme Martin. She sounded so small and pathetic after all that had happened. Somehow, the very trees seemed louder than her. I squeezed Alice's wrist and turned slowly to face her, not sure what I was expecting. The twisted, all too perfect face of somebody else? Or the gruesome visage of her true nature? I don't think I was breathing, but by the time I'd turned about, all I saw was Esme. Esme in her silly heart print pyjamas, the fabric all torn, smudged with earth. Her eyes were wild and glassy. I couldn't count her freckles beneath the dirt streaked over her cheeks.

"Oh my god," she squeaked out. She stepped to us, wrapping her arms about us both in a claustrophobic embrace. Alice was as stiff as me. "Oh my god, it's really you two. You've *no* idea how glad I am to see you —"

"Esme?" Alice ventured. Her voice was flat. I felt my girlfriend freeze against us. She pulled back slowly, taut as an elastic band, her face paler and wary.

"What? Why are you looking at me like that, the both of you?" Ping pong, her eyes going back and forth between us. Dark blue, I noted, like they always had been. I was looking for every small detail I could remember about her. One corner of her mouth drooped a little lower than the other. She said it was from how she slept on her left side all the time. Had I exaggerated it in memory? I didn't know what to think. "Please don't look at me like that. God, *say* something."

"Is it really you?" My own voice cracked, pathetically. Would somebody who was pretending to be someone else be honest about it all? Had Esme really turned into someone else? Was she even still human? She looked desperately over me, her bottom lip quivering.

"Who the fuck *else* would I be?" The wail of the snake-child in the distance cut her off. She grabbed our hands instinctively, squeezing so hard I felt my knuckles crack. Alice winced. "Oh, gawd. You hear that, too, right? Tell me you hear that, too."

"We hear that, too." Alice tried to pull her hand away. It slid in Esme's fingers and her sister blinked at her, confused. "Esme. What's going on?"

"Why do you think *I* know?"

"Esme, we've been running from you. For days. You've been... you've been —"

"Why would you *run* from me?" Her voice was growing higher, shriller with desperation. "Please don't fucking abandon me here again. I know that look. That's your *I'm going to fucking book it* look."

"Calm down," I snapped. This time, I was the one who didn't let go of her hand. "What do you remember over the last couple of days, Esme? Do you remember anything at all?" She stared at me, moon-faced. She seemed so different from the confident, sure-footed girl I remembered, but I don't think I was very much the same either, after all I'd seen.

"I don't — I remember — I mean, we fought, I think? About the board games. You all drinking." She brushed over it like it was nothing. Like she hadn't absolutely humiliated Cannon that night. I exchanged a glance with Alice.

"What else?"

"I don't know! Why are you interrogating me, exactly?" The breath caught in her throat. "What do you mean... what did you mean when you said you've been running from me?"

"Hey, easy solution," Alice gushed, pressing herself closer to us when the snake-child sang again. "How do you feel about ripping people's throats out?"

"*What?*"

"Answer the question!"

"Uh... it's highly fucking illegal?"

That was a good enough answer for me, and most importantly, it was the kind of answer my girlfriend would have given on a brighter, nicer day. I grabbed Alice's hand, too. In this little triangle, we all bent our heads together. "We have food in our bags," I hissed out quickly, "and we're — we're trying to find everyone else —"

" — we have to get help," Alice cut in. "We're going to make a run for it, out of the woods, and get help. Right, Hana?"

"Right. Yeah. We keep getting lost, right? In the trees, Esme? You were lost?"

She nodded her head, her eyes rabbit-bright.

"We're going to fucking book it. If you see a tree that's been marked by a — by a shirt sleeve or whatever, we go the other way. Got it?"

"Okay. Okay, that's a shit plan."

"It's all we've got." I appealed to her with my eyes, which probably looked like sheer lunacy to her. "You stick with me, okay? Okay, baby?"

At the familiarity of the pet name, the bygones behind us, Esme's face softened. She nodded, once, twice — a third time, quicker. We all held hands like we were pre-schoolers in a line, trafficked across the road. We all breathed in together. At the next snake's wail, we all booked it, crashing through the trees.

We didn't let each other go.

Esme

Finn Armstrong sat within the dead wood of the cabin, regaling his new audience with our story so far. He left out the most lurid details, of course, because he was afraid that if he didn't, they would laugh him off. Worse, what do you do with a lunatic? You cast him out of your home, because madness is contagious. If they removed him, he had nowhere else to run, except to another cabin — and there were so many trees between. We could still catch him.

Not that he knew that I was in the trees, or the wood, or the floor, or the ceiling. He pictured a cryptid, pale and sleek — a form that looked like mine, but was twisted to a grotesque mockery. It wasn't that he couldn't remember how I had appeared to him, but that in order to reconcile things with his sanity, he had to recall me as far more deformed than I was. If he remembered Esme Martin and I as one and the same, he was afraid his lunacy would become very, very real. Then, they would be justified in throwing him out.

So, he told a measured story of a teenage girl turned murderer. He whittled down the repeating, mocking woods as a group of college kids lost with zero survival skills. The couple and the boys listened and watched with varying levels of fluency and sympathy, but his tone convinced them of one thing — there was something awful happening in the woods, and there might be more to worry about in there than just a girl. The older man scratched his forehead under the brim of his cap — he hadn't yet taken it off — and turned to his wife with a bit of a flustered demeanour. "I think you should take the car," he said, and her face immediately puckered with worry. They had open, earnest faces, hard-working with sun damage. Her cheeks, perpetually pink, turned ever redder.

"And then what will you do?" she asked in the child-language that Finn couldn't understand. The man breathed in and hauled up his shoulders, and one of the more practical boys with bright, sharp eyes corrected him.

"You both should go. We'll go into the woods with him. Help him find his friends." He said this in clear, enunciated English, empathising with the feverishly confused expression on Finn's face. Finn immediately straightened.

"We have to go prepared. We could get lost. We might… I mean, we might run into an animal. I think there were animals out there."

The group exchanged a look. The boy most fluent in English smiled faintly at Finn and inclined his head. "We've been in the woods," he said gently. "We know our way around. We can take — weapons? To defend ourselves?" He looked around his peers to see how much they agreed to this, and they all nodded, excited to play warriors. The older couple huffed and looked bothered. "You take the car and get some help," he repeated again to them. "They'll need help."

It was an understatement. Finn hadn't been brave enough to say he'd watched two of his friends die, but he'd alluded to some grievous bodily harm. All the more reason to be wary of animals in the woods. He sat, bathing in guilt, as he watched these kind boys his age, or slightly older, good-naturedly offering their aid to a stranger. He thought that a better person would tell them all the details, and he thought he'd *been* that better person. He *was* afraid that if he was that better person, he'd lose them, and he'd lose all hope of salvaging what little of his friends remained.

So, he sat in silence, his hands braced on his bare knees, covering where the skin had been scraped by low-hanging branches, or from when he had stumbled running and half-skidded across the earth and the knotted roots. When he looked down, the cuts were on the backs of his hands, too, webbing across his knuckles. He seemed surprised to see them, like maybe they should have separated from him. Some of the blood had sprayed across his shirt, too, drying down into a dark, clinging stain.

He realised that that was probably why the couple were huffing and dragging their feet, and why the younger boys' eyes were lit with feverish curiosity. They weren't scared of his story. They were, in fact, scared of *him*.

Her feet had grown numb hours ago, though she still felt the occasional biting pain at her ankles. She'd lost count of the cuts on her legs. The low-hanging branches nipped and nipped and nipped, taking small sacrifices with every step. The trees had grown closer; Elsa couldn't remember seeing such dense forestry near their cabin. How far had she stumbled along in her shocked stupor? The moss rounded up to meet her like small mountains. Just a little further, she kept telling herself. We let her go.

Between the closely clustering pillars of the trees, she started to see the light. It squeezed around the bark, fluttering to her eyelashes in a whispering promise. The moss and close-packed earth began to give way to loosely waving grass. Even the air seemed to change. It smelled more — *open*. She pushed her legs harder, twitching agony back down to her heels. Frustrated, she began using her hands, pulling herself forward. The blood had long dried on her palms.

What would she do when she found another cabin? She forced her mind to work, gritting her teeth, pulling each tendril of thought back into the black hole where cognitive thought had been. She would ask for help. How? With words. Words, appealing words. She had dead friends. Her friends had died in the woods. Please help. *Please help.* The trees started opening up, the ground sloping downward. Her heel slid and she scraped down a slanting rock. It took the skin off the sole of her foot — when had she lost her sandal? — and grated up her spine. She cried out, frustrated, tears springing from the corners of her eyes. Suddenly, it seemed impossible to sit back up. The blouse beneath her cardigan was suctioned to her chest from the matting blood — *Cannon's* matting blood. She saw his pale, sightless eyes watching her, begrudging. She dug her fingers into the dirt, willing it to push her back up.

She stared up at the trees, at me. I wondered if she saw me. I felt more like a ghost than before. She filled up her shallow rising chest, gripped the earth, and I could hear her hiss.

"*Crawl*," she growled to herself. And she crawled. She flipped onto her belly and turned herself about, dragging her stomach over the rock face that had tripped her. The skin of the roots skinned her elbows. The pain was temporary. She had to leave the woods. The same instinct that caused man to run from his first predator, it told her she had to leave the woods. The momentum of the sloping earth started sliding her down. For a moment — just one moment — it felt like she was careening down a cliff.

She hit a tangle of roots larger than the rest. I felt the impact ricochet in my own bones, wherever they lay. She landed just perfectly, her back to the body of the tree. The tree, its large, thick body, rose tall and proud. It spread its many arms out, out, out — fingers that reached to the very end of the earth, a veil of leaves to guide them. She guided her head back and stared up, awe-struck. Afraid.

She'd found us. Finally, we weren't alone.

Alice

My sister held my hand like I hadn't tried to kill her — how many days ago? She held my hand like we were two mischievous daughters running down the stairs at our mother's wake. She held my hand like she was pushing me behind her under the disapproving glower of our uncle. She held my hand like she would always defend me like she promised. She'd promised. My sister was alive; my sister was well. I hadn't killed her. I felt like an idiot, stumbling behind her and Hana with my eyes filling up. I'd convinced myself that it was all a lost cause — that this was all because of *me*.

But she was alive!

"Keep up!" Esme snapped back at me, and I didn't even mind. I didn't mind if she called me a *fucking cunt* for the rest of my life. The trees were growing sparser. I could see the waving grass of an open meadow ahead, not a cabin in sight. We made it. We escaped the cycle of endless trees and our blood-stained cabin, over and over and over...

We burst into the open grass like sailors diving into the sea. We practically fell face first. Hana looked like she was about to plant a kiss on each individual blade. Open hills rolled upon themselves up into the skyline, interspersed only occasionally by a line of spiky trees. I could even make out little cabins. Far off, but closer than they'd seemed yesterday, or the day before. I let the tears run free, and even a stupid laugh.

"We're free!" Esme yelped, doing a little jump. "Fucking *finally*!" She collapsed atop Hana, laughing, and they embraced each other. They clung to each other, wet with sweat and blood from their little cuts. The two final girls of my vision, though instead of me, it was Esme. I felt a sudden pang of jealousy, which stopped my laughter, my happy tears. Did I really envy *her*, my sick and twisted sister? Or did I envy her for having Hana?

Hana was fierce. Hana was beautiful. Hana was, I thought, everything my sister didn't deserve to have. The nastiest part of me didn't see what Hana saw in Esme. I should have revelled in their happiness at each other's survival, but I felt it curdling bitter at the base of my stomach. Now that I knew I was in the clear, that I hadn't harmed a hair on Esme's head, all my determination to be the hero faded away. I was jaded, cynical, and this version of me would have left my sister in that cabin to rot for an eternity.

That night in the kitchen — I'd kept it at bay for as long as I could, not wanting to scrutinise it so closely. I guess I wanted to pretend to myself that I was innocent — just misunderstood. We'd been the last two awake. I'd felt out of place among all her friends. I guess I wanted the same comfort she used to give me as a kid. I felt like I was still *just* a kid. And she'd just stood there, leaning on the countertop with that dumb yellow blouse, twirling a red curl around her finger and rolling her eyes. She was a caricature.

"Oh, drop the act," she'd told me. "That whole *I'm just a kid* thing. We both know better than that, right? So, drop it."

"What does that mean?" I'd asked, the air cold at the top of my chest. She leered at me.

"I heard sweet little Alice is fucking around with people she shouldn't be. Or just *fucking* them. Didn't I tell you to stay away from Uncle Rowan? He's a fucking creep."

The air in my chest immediately turned hot. It solidified in my throat. She took my blushing as something else and let out a disgusted laugh loud enough to wake all the others. What would they do then? Line up in a row like her personal sitting ducks and laugh at me, too? I felt my eyes sting.

"Wow," she said, lifting her hands up in an *I wash myself of you* gesture. "You never fail to surprise me. Anyway, just cut the whole act —"

"I know you got an abortion."

She froze with her back to me. She'd been reaching for a knife to start to cut up some bread — a late-night sandwich. It was innocent. I don't know why she picked up the knife first. Maybe everything would have been different if she'd gone for the bread instead. Finally, she turned back, weighing the rustic little handle in her palm, her mouth twisting. I kept going. Adrenaline, I guess.

"I know it was Uncle Rowan's. You're not the only one who knows everyone's business, so... so watch your mouth."

"Are you serious?" Esme's face was completely blank. The knife was pointing at me. I looked between it and her; squared my jaw instead of backing down.

"It's not like you were willing either —"

"Shut *up*, Alice. Just shut up about it."

"Why? Why do I have to be *quiet* about it when you can throw it in my face at any moment?" My voice was climbing higher. Let her ducks come out and squawk at me. I didn't give a fuck anymore. "You knew this whole time and you've just kept it in your ammo case with everyone else's secrets? Is that it?"

"I said *shut up!*" The knife was up then, with purpose. There was no mistaking that she was threatening me, her own flesh and blood. I was just a kid. No matter what she said, I was just a kid, and I didn't have a say, and I didn't want any of it. I didn't want it, and she hadn't either. I wished she could see that. I wished she could see *me*. She took a step nearer to me, the tip of her chin puckering when her bottom lip pulled up. "You don't know the half of what I went through. You're lucky."

"Quit pointing the knife at me."

She didn't. She walked right up to me until the point of the knife was tickling under my chin. She thought it was all a game, like she always did, and she didn't care who she hurt in the process. I was so, so angry at her. I just wanted her to *stop*.

"You are *never* going to tell anyone else what you just said. Do you understand, Alice? *Never.*"

"Why? Don't you want everyone else laughing at you, too?"

She smacked me, hard and fast. I thought she was going to do worse, so I grabbed the knife from her. My cheek and jaw hurt real bad, but at least she didn't have the knife anymore. At least she wouldn't *really* hurt me. She looked shocked that I'd taken it from her, and she actually looked scared. Esme, my sister who was always the one in control, always the one pulling the strings, was now scared of *me*.

I felt powerful.

"You little slut," she said, half in disgust and half in admiration. I went to smack her back, except I didn't. I used the knife instead, didn't I? And I remember the slicing, the push against flesh — skin parts very easily. It's the meat under that gives trouble. And then the blood, of course, made a mess. It ruined my turtleneck, and it covered the kitchen. What fascinated me the most was how she crumpled, like she was weightless. So full of life and hatred one moment, and then just… gone.

For a little while, anyway.

Now she was grabbing Hana by the cheeks and kissing her in the bank of grass. It was like a painting. I realised I wasn't much better than her. I was full of hatred, too. She looked at me over her girlfriend's shoulder, her dark eyes boring right through me. Where we were covered in little scratches from running through the woods, her skin was perfectly unblemished. Even the dirt on her cheek had smudged away. There weren't any freckles there, not like I remembered there being. I was looking at a stranger again. I was looking at a stranger again and my sister was dead — always had been, and it was because of me, or because of the woods. It didn't matter in the end. I knelt slowly, reaching for a slab of rock that marked where the woods ended and the meadow began. The stranger was smiling at me.

"Alice," Hana said, her shoulders relaxed, a momentary respite. "Alice, we made it —" And she paused, seeing me lift up the rock. Her face dropped in horror and bitter disappointment.

"That's not Esme," I said, struggling to keep my voice even. The rock was heavy in my hands. "Hana, that's not her." I begged her to see what I saw — to not let her relief blind her. She was shaking her head. She already didn't believe me, and not-Esme just *stared* at me. "Hana, please, that's not her."

"I defended you. I thought what happened in the kitchen was an accident."

"It was! It was, Hana. But that's not her —"

"We *just* got her back," she said forcefully. "We *just* found her. Tell her, Esme. Tell her it's you." She looked to the stranger, but the stranger was looking away across the meadow. Cresting the hill was another figure, but it wasn't standing. It crawled across the ground, slithering almost like a snake. One hand in front of the other, fingers pulling taut around tufts of grass, sometimes pulling them up. The face was covered in blood, and so was the cardigan.

I dropped the rock.

ESMIE

Esmie

If it were a race, Elsa would have won her gold. She'd have won bouquets of flowers for a lifetime. At least five fucking trophies. Sure, there was no one else *in* the race, but that wasn't the point.

Her sheer fucking determination was beautiful.

She pulled herself bit by bit over the sloping meadow. She hadn't spotted a single cabin because she hadn't been elevated enough to see them spread over the hills below. Desperate times brought desperate tunnel vision. It was awful luck to have freed herself from the woods, only to drive herself towards them again — but there we were, standing between her and hopelessness. Maybe she didn't believe her eyes, not fully, because she kept crawling anyway. Maybe she saw me and was determined to ignore me to save her own life. Hana had stood up. Alice had forgotten the rock and stumbled forward towards Elsa. The both of them didn't know what to do. They'd have helped her up, maybe, but they looked at her feet and saw soles matted with blood — her own this time — and an ankle turned a sickening way from her fall down the slope. Elsa didn't feel that particular ache. That was another saving grace for her.

"Elsa," Hana called from far away. I felt sad that she'd already turned her focus from me, but that was a distant feeling. Coming nearer at hand was the hunger, the terrible hunger, and I was glad that Hana hadn't been alone when it came. If I could have done anything to spare her, anything at all,

I would have. No possession nor curse nor woods of the land would ever convince me not to spare Hana Baily. She turned toward me and, despite how much she wanted not to, she saw then what I was, who I wasn't, and a part of her that had been persevering through sheer spite broke. I thought I heard it, like a seashell cracking on the wind. I walked past her, then knelt. I extended a hand and rested it in Elsa's dark, wind-tossed hair.

"Is it over?" Elsa mumbled. She looked up at me through the mask of Cannon's blood, her eyes dull and gone. She couldn't see me clearly. She only saw the ghost. I caressed her cheek and smiled. I'd done that before once upon a time, when her shoulders were shaking and her heart was breaking. I'd caressed her cheek and held her close and told her it was okay. I had the videos. *I had the videos.* And she had tensed against me before the high, warring cry — the hatred that broke us apart.

"It's over," I told her. My hand lightly chucked her chin. It went lower and closed about her neck, so slender and white. Hana was screaming at me to stop, then. I wish I could have told her about the all-consuming hunger, explained myself, but I suppose there was nothing that could ever exonerate me.

It wasn't quick and easy, but I wanted to show Elsa that she'd nearly made it. I wanted to show her the small red cabins that blanketed the meadows, and how, in another life, she'd have crawled to one of them and been driven to a hospital where she would have survived. It would have been okay. She was the sort of person who would find peace in that. I was annoyed when she struggled instead — stubborn to the end, her fingers prying at my hand as it clasped about her throat, hard enough to leave bruises. I jerked my wrist and felt the bone snap. There — a second mercy. A quick kill with no joy to it. The girls screamed behind me, small superficial noises. All that mattered was the hunger. When I pulled my hand back, she floated in the air, head permanently cocked like an irritated sparrow. Her eyes stared, blind. I was taken for a moment by her. She looked like a sculpture.

Then came the shove. I flopped like a fish down onto the grass, my head bouncing off the packed earth. It would have really hurt, once upon a time. Hana was standing above me, between me and the hovering corpse. Her eyes were wide and wild. *Don't look at me like that,* I wanted to say. *Get out of the way,*

I also wanted to say. I wanted to taste Elsa's blood on my tongue. I wanted to fill the hunger so that I didn't hurt her, the girl I really, really liked. I saw a second-hand bookstore with printed posters papered up the walls — old musty bindings stacked so high they looked like a staircase. There stood a girl with a dark fringe and a stubby ponytail, and she was thumbing through *Dracula*, a contemplative wrinkle to her nose. She was looking down at me now and crying, exasperated and despairing, the air catching in her throat, her chest rising and falling, hyperventilating.

"What did you do with her!" she yelled at me. Then she kicked me. The shock of it rang through my stomach. "What did you do with fucking *Esme*, you fucking *piece of shit!*" So, she no longer saw me in turn. I saw her everywhere, but she no longer saw me. I felt the hunger growl and coil up my throat. My sister pulled at her arm, tugging her back, her survival instincts prevailing. Hana jerked away, then turned and marched back toward that slab of rock. Her spine was all tensed up, taut and sinewy like a leather band all the way up. She smelled of the same desperation Elsa had had towards the end.

"It's your fault," I told Alice. "It didn't have to be this way. You ruined everything." Her small, pointed face had gone white as the sky above. She didn't even twitch at my taunt.

"I wish I'd finished the job," she said to me. A conversation between two sisters. Who would have thought? Our mother would be turning in her grave. Our father would throw up in the bathroom like he did after he had one too many whiskeys to forget the sorrows. What a disappointment we both were, in the end. Hana hefted up the slab of rock and I could hear her sobbing from where I lay.

"You weren't the only victim," I said. "You know that. But you never had to bear the fruit of it. You never had to feel it grow inside of you."

"I didn't let it turn me into a monster, either."

"We can go back to it," I continued calmly. "Together. We can make a little fucked up family. Start from the beginning again, before anything ever came between us." She looked down at me, frowning, not quite understanding. If I strained my ears, I could hear its song coming nearer, winding through the trees. She tilted her head and listened, too.

"Alice, get out of the way." Hana's lean arms were straining around the flat rock. Her eyes were bright white dots in her face. I thought it would be nice to die by her hand. I knew she'd make it fast and easy. "Alice!"

But Alice didn't get out of the way. She turned to face the trees like she was in a dream, standing in the shadow of Elsa's hovering body. We were all in a nightmare, but I realised then, just then, that we weren't really. That this was all real, and I had killed my friends, and I was going to kill them, too. Her long straight hair shifted in the breeze — the meadow sighed, once.

Then I could just hear the singing.

alice

Our mum had looked more like Esme than she did me. The round face, the wavy instead of straight hair. I remember that she was open and warm and tired. She was always very tired. She would wait up for dad at the kitchen table, a nostalgic silhouette. She'd stir her cup with the teabag, one manicured finger extended, tugging on the string that was soggy from steam. She got in an accident when she went to a ski resort with her girlfriends. She hit her head, got a brain bleed, and was hooked up in the hospital overnight before she passed. When dad came home, it was like he'd inherited her tiredness on top of his own. The house grew a lot emptier after that.

Our sisterhood suffered for that, too. At first, it seemed like it'd go the other way. At her wake, Esme squeezed my hand in her loose-fitting black dress, her perfume a sugary, caramelised lemon. She leaned close to me and whispered, "We'll take care of each other, all right?" I'd believed her, stupidly, not knowing it would all change once she went off to college. She was free, then, and she began to resent her oath to me. She would come home on breaks and regale me with all the gossip and secrets she collected to herself like trinkets, but that was the only special privilege I seemed to receive. One night, she caught our uncle Rowan looking at me sideways, leering, and she sucked in her lips and leered at me, too — like I was disgusting. Like I reminded her of her.

I tried to tell her. She told me she'd take care of me, so I went to her. She wouldn't let me get the words out. She held up her hand and said, "Hasn't this fucking family been through enough?" Like I was the one who personally shoved our mother down the slope, spinning out of control. I watched our dad come home from another shift at the hospital and I closed myself up, a stuck zipper. If Esme didn't want to hear it, dad would want to hear it even less. Sometimes, I pretended at night that mum was in the room with me, and I'd whisper it to her. She'd just sit there, though, just out of my sight, spinning the string of the teabag on the tip of her nail. *I don't know what to do, love,* I could hear her say. *I'm dead and gone.* As for the abortion, I'd always been sort of aware of it. I'd seen the pamphlets for the clinic in Esme's room. I took it for granted. It's the kind of thing you only put two and two together once you were a little older and wiser. I kept it in my back pocket like my sister did with all *her* secrets. I guess I envied that she was so in control of herself and everyone else. I thought if I could exert a little power over her, too, then that meant I was at the top of the pyramid.

It was a pretty sorry pyramid.

It felt like the threads of my back pocket had come undone, finally. The singing grew closer, and it seemed very familiar — *bone*-familiar. Like a lullaby mum had sung to us once upon a time, when we were really little. I pictured her in the afterlife, holding up the thing that would have been Esme's baby. Not an actual living creature, just a collection of clot and flesh. I pictured her nursing it until it turned into a snake, viscous and oily. I imagined her looking at me and shrugging. *I'm dead and gone,* would be her excuse, *and it was never alive anyway.* The singing came nearer. Hana was saying something, but I couldn't hear her over that sound.

The trees parted. The snake had found us at last.

Esme

They walked through the cabin like it was made of broken glass, Finn loitering at the rear. He felt like there should be crime scene tape. Maybe he should have a safety blanket wrapped about his shoulders. Instead of law enforcement though, a group of Swedish college boys led the tentative procession inside holding bats or rolling pins or, for some reason, one of them had found a rake. Finn followed at the end, feeling like he should be in front; feeling like he should take ownership somehow. He stepped slowly into the hallway, which led to the bathroom, Elsa and Alice's room also down a little ways from it. There was a scrape of blood on the wall which led to the door, and he supposed it was Kaida's, in a horrible, benumbed way. The boys started to spread out, easing once they realised nobody else was in the cabin.

Well, we were watching, but they wouldn't know that.

"Did the animal do that?" the bright-eyed, English-speaking one asked Finn, pointing at the wall. He didn't know how to answer that, even though he knew it wasn't an animal.

"I don't know," he finally managed, and the boy frowned. A heavily enunciated *holy shit* echoed from further into the cabin. They ended up following suit instead of puzzling out the rest of the wall. There were many more blood streaks in the dining area and a lot more visible in the kitchen. The fridge doors had been left open, and water was pooling into the floorboards.

The boys were sifting through broken plate shards, blinking at the overturned stools. Finn had to admit, it *did* look like some wild animal had charged through and decimated the whole group of them.

"Do you think any of your friends came back?" the English-speaking one queried further, even though he didn't look convinced as he said it. If any of them had come back, they'd have seen them by now. Finn stared at the open fridge doors, trying to remember if they'd been left that way. If the struggle with Esme had somehow thrown them open. He looked closer at the water pooling between the floorboards. The dark stains swept in a long line outwards, like something had been dragged out of the shelves. It was a peculiar sight.

"That's a lot of blood," one of the other boys said, scratching his head. "We should probably — I mean, maybe we should leave this to the police."

"How long will that take?" Finn stumbled out. "My friends are still out there, they're still — I mean, they're still at risk." The boys all exchanged an unsure glance.

"I don't think there are a lot of wild animals about," the one who had stuck by Finn's side said carefully. "At least, no bears, or wolves, or…" He quietly ran out of what else could have left such carnage behind. Finn opened his mouth, then closed it again. Whatever he said, it would sound completely made up.

"I just don't think they're safe out there in the woods. This sounds crazy, but — I mean, every time we tried to find help, we kept getting turned about and we'd just end up back here. And the whole time, we were… *hunted*." He looked about at his companions in mute appeal. Most of them avoided his eyes, not sure how to take it all. The one with the rake was poking at some of the blood streaks. "Listen, if you know the woods better than we do, it shouldn't be any problem, right? You can help me find the rest of them; bring them to safety."

"We should *really* wait for the police," the one with the rake said. He was finding it hard to look away from all the blood. Finn swallowed. He sought out the bright-eyed boy who was staying at his elbow, who seemed to take charge. If he could just appeal to him… what then? What if they *all* got lost in the woods again, and Esme picked them off one by one? Was it better to do nothing or to take another step into deep shit? He raised his hands, then dropped them. They came up again, hovering just in front of him, a quiet gesture that seemed to weigh the significance of what he was saying.

"Listen. This could be the difference between life and death for them, all right? Strength in numbers, right?" Somebody had said that once upon a time. It all felt so blurred and distant. "Please. We know the police are coming either way? Those two we left at the cabin, they went to get help, yeah?" He looked about for agreement and received a slow *yeah* in response. His hands gestured emphatically. "Then we could be out there, helping them, instead of, what… loitering round here? Doing nothing?" The thought genuinely made him sick. He didn't want to stay there anyway — not with all that bloody reminder of what had happened. The boys looked at one another, slowly inhaling. They already had the weapons, the guts, and the curiosity.

"All right," the bright-eyed one said. "Do you remember where in the woods you left them?"

It was a stupid fucking question. Finn knew he couldn't find the same place twice in those woods if he tried.

But he said yes anyway.

Hana

I watched it happen in slow motion. One moment she was there, staring at the woods, and the next she was gone. With a lurch of oil-slick scales, a glimpse of mottled pink cheek meat, the snake swallowed her whole — well, nearly whole. I could see her feet, briefly. Soft green flip-flops that had been scuffed and discoloured by dirt. The snake reared its head back — once, twice — and then those were gone, too.

Alice was gone.

I screamed. Load of good that did. I screamed and I screamed, and I dropped the slab of rock a long moment ago. I was just kneeling on the grass, screaming. My fingers had curled into tight fists. I couldn't feel the nails breaking the skin of my palms. I screamed and I screamed and at some point, I guess, the snake was gone — or had never been there. Maybe I'd hallucinated it all. But the giant fucking snake was gone, and so was Alice. I hadn't hallucinated *that*.

Nor had I hallucinated Esme. She lay in the grass, still as the moment I'd shoved her down. She stared up at the sky, and the sky reflected back in the depths of her eyes. I say it was Esme, but I know it wasn't now — it wasn't, and it never was, and I can never be sure when it stopped being her. All I know is that *thing* took and it took and it took, and it was never contented. I knew it would take me next, and there would be no end to it. It would swallow the whole world if it could.

"What are you waiting for?" I groaned. My throat felt ruptured from all the screaming. "Here I am. Are you going to finish the job or not?" The eyes fluttered, dark auburn lashes ruffling as she slid her gaze toward me. There was no change in her expression otherwise. No grief. No malice. God, I'd have felt better if there *was* malice. "What, are you just going to lie there? After everything?"

"Everything?" she repeated, like an echo. I felt the rage boil inside of me.

"*Everything*. Kaida, Byron, Elsa, Alice — you've killed them all, haven't you? Is that all you're going to do now? Fucking *lie down* and bask in it?" Again, the eyes fluttered, like a blink but not a blink. Her hands were clasped over her belly. She could have been getting ready for stargazing for all I knew.

"I'm not lying down," she told me. "I'm not anywhere, doing anything. I'm long gone, I think, if I was ever here at all." The cryptic bullshit was worse than if she'd, I don't know, *hissed*. I stared at her, repulsed, contemptuous. I wanted to pick up the rock again and slam it on her face, over and over. I wanted to kill, too. To take revenge. What an ugly thing to feel towards someone — some*thing* — you once loved. I stared at her, my hands shaking, waiting for my judgement to fall. Slowly, she sat up. She looked back toward the woods.

"What are the most beautiful words you know?" She was talking to herself. "'I love you'?"

I craned my neck back, trying to see what she was seeing — what she was talking about. The trees stared back at me, quiet and morose as ever, with no sign of the snake, no sign really that there had been any violence at all. When I looked back, she had laid down again. I crawled to her side, desperate to have her look into my face, desperate to get my answers.

Elsa stared back at me from the grass, her head perpetually cocked, lips parted on a scream that had never come.

ESME

Esme

They found Hana cradling Elsa's body. She didn't respond when they called out to her. She just held the dead girl close, her knuckles white with how tight she clasped those cold, unresponsive arms. Finn reeled back when he saw what had happened — Elsa covered in Cannon's blood, her neck and ankle snapped. The boys with him tried to stir Hana to no avail. "Can we carry her back?" one of them asked. The whites of all their eyes were rabid and showing. This was the first time any of them had seen a dead body up close. A dead body that had clearly died in torment, at that.

Finn couldn't answer.

They did, though, in the end. They pried her hands loose and hoisted her up by the arms, and her feet sort of started working. Her body was present, but her mind wasn't. She was locked inside. And even when Finn whispered to her, slid his shoulder under her armpit, she wouldn't even blink. Tears coursed from her eyes, and nobody could tell if it was grief or a physical response to her staring. Nobody knew what to do with the dead body, either. They decided to leave it for the police. Even without all the tape, they knew it was a crime scene.

It would take hours for the middle-aged couple to come back with help. They didn't want to go back to the cabin full of blood, so they went to the couple's instead and shuffled Finn and Hana inside like they were inmates. When the door was closed, you could just see their heads bobbing outside the windows, sometimes peeking in. There was lots of shaking, lots of thumbing at their noses. Soft, muttered Swedish that theorised and recoiled from the potential truth. Finn sat on the floral cushions of a replica Gustavian sofa, his hands clasped numbly between his thighs. He wouldn't leave Hana's side. I think deep down, she was thankful for that. Sometimes, he would look at the profile of her face and open his mouth, then decided better, and would sink back into his own solitary quiet.

We watched.

The couple returned with a small patrol and a pair of medics, their faces wary and taut from not knowing what to expect. When they saw Finn inside with his shirt all torn and covered in blood, their expressions turned grim and routine. The medics looked both the youths over, and Hana began to stir. Something about all the new faces, the noise, the cleanliness. It told her that she wasn't in the woods anymore — that her feet had stopped running and her heart palpitations had evened out. She unfurled her hands and stared at her palms and fingers like she didn't recognise herself.

The police looked over their cabin and found a ransacked abode with a small stash of drugs. They took two statements from two college kids obviously in shock, both of whom were hesitant to tell the truth. Finn said something about animals. It could be cut and dry — maybe a bear happened upon the cabin. The youths, all drugged up, all paranoid, went a little crazy. Ran out into the unfamiliar woods, got lost, fucked themselves up. Then they looked at Elsa's body and saw the bruises on her neck shaped like fingertips. Suddenly they were looking sideways at Hana and Finn. They were chewing the insides of their cheeks, writing things down, and handling them like contaminated evidence. They were shuffled into the patrol car together. Shoulder to shoulder in the backseat, stinking of days' worth of layered sweat, they finally met each other's eyes.

"Hey," Finn said. He wet his lips with the tip of his tongue. The corners of his mouth were cracked from days without water. The tips of the trees had left little scratches on his high cheekbones.

"Hey," Hana answered. She looked over him quietly. The patrolman hemmed and hawed outside the car, having a last word or two with the middle-aged couple — their star witnesses. The younger boys were all scrambled and confused. Traumatised. The two of them could see their midriffs swaying from side to side just outside the glass of the passenger window. The patrolman's stomach stuck out a good inch over the waist of his trousers, his dark shirt pulled taut over it.

"You all right?" Finn tried again. He didn't make eye contact this time. Maybe he thought it would be easier to hold a conversation if he didn't. Hana contemplated the question for a little while, her thumb making soft, scuffing sounds as she fidgeted.

"No. You?"

"*Nah.*"

They looked at each other again. "How'd you get away?" Hana asked, strangely casual in the confines of a police vehicle. The corner of Finn's mouth twitched despite himself. It didn't last long.

"Just ran, you know? Kept running until I came out the other end."

"I wonder why the woods let you out." They didn't question that statement — the assumption that the woods had been acting of their own free will. At some point over those last few hours, they stopped seeing the entity as Esme, instead as something older and deeper in the ground than her. It had no name. It likely predated names. Finn cocked his head, his eyes roaming back to the patrolman's quivering belly.

"I don't know. I think we were the odd ones out, you and I. I can't think of a secret she might have had on me. Nothing that'd ruin my life, anyway." He paused. "Maybe that's why we're the last two."

"Last two?"

"Yeah, um. It got Cannon as well. And I guess you never found Byron."

Hana paused, then shook her head. "Not a trace. It must have been hungry."

"You figure that's what it did? Eat them?" They both kept an eye on the patrolman. It was a forbidden conversation, really. Discussing the crimes at hand, attributing them to the supernatural. Wouldn't hold up in a court of law, would it? "Why d'you think that?"

"I don't know. Maybe I'm just thinking that way because I'm starving."

He looked at her, surprised that she could still have an appetite. Maybe that was a good thing, in the end. "I'm glad you made it out without a scratch, Baily," he said. He paused and looked her over again. Her tank-top was torn from their trek through the woods as he remembered it being. Her hair was tousled, her cheeks, knees, and elbows streaked with dirt. He searched for signs of any other injury — any telling blood, hers or her own, that seeped through the black material. His thoughts kept snagging on the trees and their greedy branches. *Hungry* was right, actually. The trees nipped and nipped, nibbled and nibbled, taking bits and pieces of their flesh and blood. She looked back at him, too, her slender brows lifting. Under the dirt, her skin shone smooth and unblemished, highlighted only by the slightest sheen of sweat.

She really had made it out without a scratch. In fact, she looked perfect.

Emma's poetry has appeared on PULP and Suburban Witchcraft, and her short fiction in literary magazines *Ginosko Literary Journal* and *The Gravity of the Thing*. Though she grew up in Japan as a mix of writer, artist, and dancer, she has moved to Scotland and has settled down fully as a scribbler, both of words and of images. She spends her days satisfying the whims of her void-shaped familiar, also known as a black cat, Treacle.

Wilson-Kanamori Emma

www.ingramcontent.com/pod-product-compliance
Lightning Source LLC
LaVergne TN
LVHW041917070526
838199LV00051BA/2646